"You want revenge," Sirena accused

"It's not *my* fault we're still married, Noah."

"I'm not seeking revenge," he insisted. "I want us to mend our rifts so we can finally write an end to this chapter and move on with our lives."

Sirena wasn't convinced that he felt so strongly about repairing their rifts. He hadn't made any effort to come after her two years ago. In fact, hadn't she waited in breathless anticipation for just that eventuality? She pushed the question away and asked, "Just how much time are we talking about?"

"I want a month," he said, some of the tension leaving his body at her apparent surrender.

"Okay," she agreed reluctantly, "but only if you don't try to seduce me into your bed. We don't have any problems in that area to be resolved."

He nodded, but she wasn't satisfied. "You'll shake on that?"

"No seduction scenes," he said, extending one hand. He slipped the other behind his back and crossed his fingers.

Carin Rafferty's inspiration for *I Do, Again* came when her husband decided to pursue blacksmithing as a hobby. It's lust at first sight for her heroine, Sirena, when she spots hero Nick toiling over an anvil. Carin's husband has further contributed to her career because his job allows them to move frequently. She feels that meeting new people and being exposed to new lifestyles and environments greatly enhances her writing. They live in Pennsylvania with their four cats.

Though *I Do, Again* is Carin's first Harlequin Temptation, her publishing history includes a Harlequin American Romance and two romances written under the name Allyson Ryan.

Books by Carin Rafferty
HARLEQUIN AMERICAN ROMANCE
320–FULL CIRCLE

I Do, Again
CARIN RAFFERTY

Harlequin Books

TORONTO • NEW YORK • LONDON
AMSTERDAM • PARIS • SYDNEY • HAMBURG
STOCKHOLM • ATHENS • TOKYO • MILAN

To Laura Bowen, Kassie Keefer
Ida Lawver, Linda Lucas
and Martha McLemore,
for making writing in Pennsylvania
so much fun!

Published January 1990

ISBN 0-373-25381-8

1

"SIRENA, YOU AREN'T divorced," Jonathan Harcourt announced without preamble as he stormed into Sirena Barrington's office and tossed her divorce decree onto her desk in an uncharacteristic display of temper.

Sirena leaned back in her chair and stared up at him. In all the years she'd known him, it was the first time she'd ever seen Jonathan agitated. She was so intrigued by this facet of his personality that she ignored his words for the moment and studied him assessingly.

Jonathan was more than her attorney. They'd been dating off and on for the past year, and during the past six months it had been more on than off. She knew he wanted their casual relationship to progress to something much more serious, but Sirena had been oddly reluctant for it to do so, and she wasn't certain why. Despite the fact that Jonathan was nearly fifteen years her senior, she had come to the conclusion that he would be the ideal husband for her. They shared the same social and economic background. Their interests in everything from politics to movies meshed perfectly. He understood and approved of her work at Barrington Foundation, an organization she'd founded, and one that dealt with everything from cruelty to animals to shelters for the homeless.

When she told Jonathan that she wanted to secure the foundation's future, he'd been the one to suggest setting up a trust fund. That was when he'd asked for her divorce decree; he had to verify that no one from her past had any

legal claim on her money. The only person who could have
even a remote claim on it was her ex-husband, Noah
Samson.

Now Jonathan was saying that she wasn't divorced, and
Sirena knew it wasn't true. Two years ago she'd hightailed
it to Mexico to make sure she got rid of Noah as quickly
as possible, and she'd been counting her blessings ever
since.

"Don't be ridiculous, Jonathan. Of course I'm divorced." She lifted the divorce decree and waved it at him.
"I have the document right here to prove it."

Jonathan dropped into a chair in front of her desk and
regarded her with an expression that was half sympathetic and half chastising. "You have a document, but it
isn't a divorce decree. It might as well be a recipe for taco
filling."

"A recipe for taco filling?" Sirena repeated incredu-
lously. Then she laughed. "That's a great joke, Jonathan.
You really had me going for a minute."

"I am not joking," Jonathan stated dryly. Then he raked
his hand through his immaculately styled blond hair.

That was another uncharacteristic gesture, and Sirena
frowned. He couldn't be serious, but he sure looked serious. "Jonathan, this doesn't make any sense."

"Of course it makes sense," Jonathan muttered disgruntledly. "You were the perfect mark. You didn't speak
the language. You were so desperate you probably asked
the bellhop to refer you to the appropriate officials, and
he saw the opportunity to make a quick buck. I'd bet he
even hand-delivered you to the so-called officials after he
got off duty."

When Sirena's blush gave affirmation to his scenario,
Jonathan sighed heavily. His green eyes were dark with
frustration when he asked, "Why did you go to Mexico,

Sirena? Why didn't you just come home and file for divorce?"

"It's complicated," Sirena said as she rose to her feet and crossed to her office window. It gave a beautiful view of the wide Susquehanna River that flowed sedately through the city of Harrisburg, Pennsylvania's state capital.

As she watched sunlight dance across the water, her mind flew back over the years providing her with such a clear image of the first moment she'd laid eyes on Noah Samson that she could have been lost in a time warp.

SHE'D BEEN VISITING her second cousin in Bedford, Pennsylvania, and Maggie had insisted on taking her to visit Old Bedford Village, a re-creation of pioneer America that reflected the life-styles of the area during the middle 1790s.

Though Sirena rarely enjoyed anything touristy, she had found the village fascinating. They'd wandered through original log homes where volunteers explained how the pioneers lived, and craft shops where they'd watched a weaver, a candle maker and a tinsmith ply their trades. Then they'd walked into the blacksmith shop, and as Sirena peered through a crack in the crowd, her heart had skipped a beat.

Noah had been standing in front of the blacksmith forge, bare to the waist and jeans hanging low on his hips. Sweat glistened on his massive hair-covered chest and muscled arms, all of which were covered with a fine layer of coal dust as dark as the hair on his head. She'd caught her breath when he pulled out a piece of red-hot steel, placed it into a vise and explained the steps he was taking as he molded it into a dinner gong. Then he'd thrown it into a wooden bucket of water to temper it, turned to face the crowd and, with arms akimbo and feet braced apart, asked if there were any questions. The ones trembling on

Sirena's lips as she stared at that gorgeous hunk of mas-
culinity had been: When do you get off work and would
you like to see my etchings?

She'd stood in the background, listening to the rumble
of his deep voice as he patiently answered questions and
sold engraved horseshoes and dinner gongs. As the crowd
thinned, Sirena moved forward, ready to purchase his
entire stock just to get near him.

Without looking up from the lettering he was doing, he
nodded toward a piece of paper and a pencil and told her,
"Write down what you want to buy and the name you
want engraved on it. I'll be with you in a minute."

Sirena obediently wrote down her first name and waited
as he finished his order. He pulled the paper toward him,
read it and then glanced up at her. Sirena's entire body
went into nuclear meltdown.

From afar the man was gorgeous. Up close his rugged
good looks made him positively mouth watering. His ra-
ven hair was thick and tumbled rakishly across his forehead. His eyes were a dark indigo-blue, framed with black
lashes so thick Sirena would have given away her entire
fortune to have a pair of them for herself. There was a
small jagged scar on the ridge of one high cheekbone, and
the uneven symmetry of his nose bragged that it had been
broken a time or two. But it was his lips that mesmerized
her. They looked deliciously sensual and absolutely sin-
ful when they curved into a satyr's grin as his gaze swept
over her in a blatant male appraisal that made her toes curl
in her sneakers.

"Is this your name?" he asked. When she nodded, he
said, "I've never seen it before. What nationality is it, and
what does it mean?"

Sirena had to gulp three times to find her voice. "It's
Greek. It means singing mermaid."

His eyes raked boldly over her again. "Do you sing, mermaid?"

"Only if there isn't a living soul within a mile. I'm tone-deaf."

His laugh was as sexy as the rest of him. Sirena had to grasp the rough-hewn counter in front of her to keep her knees from buckling as every feminine molecule inside her trembled in response.

When his laughter died, his eyes locked with hers and he asked, "Are you married?"

"Not the last time I checked."

"Live around here?"

"Visiting family."

"Free for dinner?"

She nodded again.

When she walked out of the blacksmith's shop, she had an engraved horseshoe, an engraved dinner gong, a dinner date and a body so hot with desire that it rivaled the steel-melting heat of Noah Samson's forge. Before the night was over, they'd made love. Thirty-six hours after that she'd become his wife. Three weeks later their marriage had ended.

"WOULD YOU LIKE ME to call the man and explain what's happened?" Jonathan asked, breaking into her reverie.

"No," Sirena stated as she turned back to face him. It was the scariest prospect she'd ever had to face in her life, but she knew that she had to be the one to break the news to Noah. "I'll call him."

But it was four days and a taco binge later before Sirena found the courage to dial Noah's number. She paled when his answering machine picked up with the message, "I'm out of town preparing for my marriage. I'll be back in three weeks."

At first, Sirena could only stare at the phone in stunned disbelief, while experiencing the oddest feeling of hurt. Then she literally panicked when she realized what old-fashioned, straitlaced, uptight Noah Samson would do to her if she let him become a bigamist.

SIRENA CURSED and slammed her fist against the steering wheel as steam rose from the front of her rental car. She pulled to the side of the road and climbed out, cursing again as antifreeze began to flood the ground. With a low cry of frustration, she kicked the front tire.

"Damn you, Noah Samson," she muttered, kicking the tire again. "Why did you have to get married out in the middle of the Maryland sticks where even Ma Bell refuses to come, instead of in your hometown like any normal human being?"

She raked her hand impatiently through her hair as she glanced up and down the deserted country road. She hadn't seen a house in miles, so there was no sense in turning back. She could only go forward. Grabbing her purse from the car, she began walking, thankful for the fact that she'd worn low-heeled sandals.

With each step she took, her frustration grew. This was a nightmare. One incredible, horrendous nightmare. If she didn't make it to the chapel on time, Noah was going to be a bigamist. She knew, however, that he wouldn't be one for long, because he'd kill her.

The thought made Sirena groan and she began to jog down the center of the graveled road. She hadn't gone far when she stumbled on loose gravel and fell to her knees. She let out a string of curses as she sat on her rump and examined her legs. Her nylons were history and her knees were as skinned as a six-year-old's.

"All this just to save your hide, Noah Samson," she muttered irritably as she climbed to her feet and began to jog again. "But I guess I do owe your blushing bride this much, though I'm sure she would have preferred a nice set of steak knives."

She kept up the pace until her chest heaved and there was a stitch in her side. She was ready to burst into tears of despair when she heard the sound of an engine behind her. Spinning around, she saw an old farm truck crawling toward her, and when it came to a stop, she hurried to the driver's window.

"My car broke down and it's important that I get to Blue Mountain Chapel as soon as possible. Can you give me a lift?"

The elderly man behind the wheel nodded as he spit a stream of tobacco juice at her feet, while four wide-eyed children peered at her over his shoulder. "As you can see, we don't have any room up front and the grandchildren are too young to ride in the back, but if you don't mind ridin' on the tailgate, I'll get you there."

"Thanks," Sirena told him gratefully, but when she arrived at the back of the truck, she released a heartfelt groan. It was filled with crates of squawking chickens and the smell was enough to make her stomach revolt. But a smelly ride was better than no ride when you were on a life-or-death mission, particularly when it was your own life that was at stake. She climbed onto the tailgate and yelled for the man to drive on.

As the truck began to bump its way down the road, Sirena glanced at her watch, noting that it was 12:45. She sent a prayer heavenward that Noah's bride was a traditionalist and had set the ceremony for two in the afternoon. That would allow Sirena enough time to get to Noah, explain what had happened and tell him that Jonathan had already filed all the necessary papers and would be pulling some strings to get the divorce processed fast. She'd then present the bride and her family with a blank check to cover all the expenses for both this wedding and the next one, then be on her merry way, provided, of course, someone would be kind enough to offer her a lift. Somehow, she didn't think it would be prudent to ask for a ride under the circumstances.

Her watch declared it to be exactly 1:00 p.m. when the truck braked to a stop and the man yelled out at her, "The chapel's at the top of those steps ahead of us."

"Thanks," she yelled back and leaped off the truck, waving at the farmer as he pulled away. Then she turned and gaped at the granite stairs that stood in front of her. There had to be fifty of them and they went straight up the side of a small mountain.

"I don't believe this!" she exclaimed as she began to climb the stairs. "I feel like the heroine in *The Perils of Pauline.*" She was thankful that at least there was only one car in the parking lot, so she didn't need to rush.

But when Sirena hit the halfway mark, she heard the musical strains of the wedding march. She couldn't believe it when the music ended immediately.

"Oh, God, please help me make it in time," she pleaded. "If you don't Noah will make sure I'm at your pearly gates before the day is out, and I'm too young to die."

Fear gave her the necessary adrenaline to take the stairs two at a time, and she gulped in deep breaths of air as she raced toward the chapel, which was surrounded by what appeared to be a thousand cars. Though her first instinct was to burst through the door, she forced herself to open and close it quietly. To her horror, the minister was saying, " . . . speak now or forever hold your peace."

It was Sirena's cue, and she knew it, but she couldn't find her voice. It was only when the minister nodded at the couple and parted his lips to continue that her vocal cords regained their function, and her "Wait!" sounded like thunder in the silent room.

As everyone in the church turned en masse toward her, Sirena nervously ran her hand over her hair and blushed when two chicken feathers drifted to the floor in front of her. She glanced at the couple sitting in the last pew, and when the woman wrinkled her nose at her, Sirena realized that she'd bought the odor of her feathery riding companions with her. At that moment she wondered if it wouldn't have been better if she'd just waited until after the ceremony and let Noah strangle her, because she wanted to do nothing more than lie right down on the floor and die from humiliation. Every well-bred Barrington female down through history had to be rolling over in her grave at this scene.

"What is it, young lady?" the minister inquired in a clearly irritated tone, and Sirena nearly turned tail and ran when she returned her gaze to the front of the church and saw Noah glaring at her.

She took a step backward and wrapped her hand around the doorknob as her eyes shifted from Noah, looking so strikingly handsome in his black tuxedo, to the petite blonde at his side, who was all decked out in white lace and satin. Even through the veil Sirena could see that the woman was beautiful, and an unexpected bolt of jealousy shot through her.

Before Sirena could begin to contemplate just what that bolt of jealousy meant, Noah said, "Sirena, I don't know what you're doing here, but there's a wedding going on. Either sit down or leave."

"I, uh, know there's a wedding going on, Noah, " she said, her voice sounding choked and high-pitched. "But I need to talk to you, and I swear that it's important. Could you, uh, step outside for a moment?"

Noah's voice took on that deceptively soft tone that meant he was furious as he said, "No, I could not step outside. Nothing could possibly be so important that it won't wait until after the ceremony."

With that, he took his bride's hands solicitously into his and turned her back toward the minister. The guests also turned, but many cast a curious glance over their shoulders at Sirena. The minister cleared his throat and parted his lips to start where he'd left off, and Sirena knew it was now or never.

"Excuse me," she said, turning the doorknob in her hand when Noah spun back around to face her, murder clearly in his eyes. She ignored him and stared at the minister as she began to ease open the door. "I'm afraid, sir, that you can't continue with this ceremony because . . . well, because Noah Samson is already married to me and my attorney says it will be at least a month before the divorce is final."

Sirena didn't wait to see what effect her announcement had on the gathering. She slipped through the door and slammed it behind her. Then she headed down those granite steps as fast as her feet could carry her, deciding that if she could reach the woods, she could hide out in them until Noah was gone. Then, when she finally got back to civilization, she'd have Jonathan contact him and deal with his wrath.

She'd almost made it to the bottom of the stairs when she heard Noah shout, "Sirena, you get your fanny back up here right this minute, or I swear I'll . . ."

Sirena didn't hear the remainder of his threat, because she'd risked a glance over her shoulder, missed the last step and hit the ground with a thud.

Stunned by the fall, she took a few seconds to recover, and by the time she pushed herself into a kneeling position, Noah's highly polished, black leather wing tips were right in front of her nose. With a sigh, she sat back on her heels, assumed her best look of martyrdom and raised her eyes to his face, deciding that if Joan of Arc could go out without a whimper, so could Sirena Angelica Barrington.

NOAH HAD NEVER BEEN as angry as he was at this very moment. No, that wasn't true, he realized as he glared down into Sirena's huge brown eyes, which seemed to fill her heart-shaped face. Her red hair was in an unruly tangle and sporting half a dozen chicken feathers, and she was peering up at him with a look that was half fear and half resignation. He'd been this angry when he came home from work a couple of years ago to find a note from Sirena stating that she was on her way to Mexico to get a quickie divorce and would Federal Express him a copy of the decree the minute she got it.

He forced himself to relax his clenched fists before glancing up the stairs at his bride, Cynthia, who asked, "Is everything all right, Noah?"

"Everything's fine, darling. You just go back into the church and I'll join you in a minute."

"All right," she said, immediately turning away.

Noah's head snapped back toward Sirena when she murmured, "Beautiful *and* obedient. It looks like you finally found the perfect woman, Noah. Congratulations."

Sirena's words stung and he shot back with, "Not all women are so insecure with themselves that they consider a man's every suggestion dictatorial, degrading and demeaning."

Sirena flinched as he repeated the words she'd thrown at him during their final argument that had sent her running for Mexico. Then she reminded herself that the three D's, as she'd come to think of them, had fit him perfectly. Noah Samson had turned out to be a full-fledged, card-carrying despot, determined to control her every move and thought, and when it didn't work, he'd dragged her to bed and kept her there until she agreed to do whatever he wanted. She parted her lips to defend herself, but decided against it. After all, she wasn't here to rehash old grievances.

"You may be right," she said as she climbed to her feet, grimacing when she put weight on her right ankle and realized she'd sprained it. She tested it and found, thankfully, it appeared to be a minor sprain. "But I don't think we need to go into that right now." She opened her purse, pulled out an envelope and handed it to him. "I recently discovered that our Mexican divorce is not legal. Inside that envelope, you'll find a copy of the divorce papers my lawyer filed on Tuesday, and he assures me that he can pull some strings and have us legally divorced within a month.

"I've also included a blank check for your bride's family," she continued when he didn't respond. "Please ask them to fill it out for the cost of today's wedding, as well as the cost of the next one, and offer them my sincere apologies for that horrible scene in the chapel. I only learned this morning where your wedding was taking place, and when I discovered that the chapel was out in the middle of nowhere with no phone service, I tried my best to get here before the ceremony started. Unfortunately, my car broke down and . . ."

Sirena stopped when she realized she was babbling and gave Noah an apologetic smile, glad to see that he no longer looked angry, though she couldn't put a name to his expression. She also realized that she'd forgotten just how handsome the man really was; he made a dashing groom. As she gazed up at him, she felt a funny little ache in the middle of her chest. Unconsciously, she reached out to straighten his lapel and smooth it against his chest, and when she felt the thump of his heart beneath her fingertips, inexplicable tears sprang to her eyes.

She glanced away from him quickly to hide them, drew in a deep breath and said, "Goodbye, Noah."

With that, she turned and limped away, unaware that Noah was staring after her in confusion. It was only when she walked around a curve in the road that he dropped his gaze to the envelope in his hand, and it finally registered that he was still married to Sirena, a tone-deaf singing mermaid, whose body had made his blood boil with passion, and whose willful, stubborn nature had made his temper explode instantaneously.

"Noah?" Cynthia called from the top of the stairs again, and Noah spun around.

As he peered up at her, he realized that she was everything he wanted in a woman. Quiet, beautiful and, he admitted reluctantly, obedient. Life with her was going to be on a smooth steady course. He gave an uncomfortable shrug of his shoulders when he realized how boring that life sounded. Feeling guilty for even having such a ridiculous thought, he hurried up the stairs.

When he reached the top, he stopped and stared down into Cynthia's questioning porcelain-blue eyes. "Everything's going to be fine," he murmured as he leaned forward and pressed a reassuring kiss to her lips. They were warm and petal-soft and complaisant beneath his, but when Noah raised his head, he found himself oddly dissatisfied with the kiss. His eyes strayed over the top of Cynthia's head to the road Sirena had taken, and he experienced a strange yearning inside that he couldn't define.

"Noah, what that woman said isn't true, is it?" Cynthia asked, drawing his attention back to her.

"I'm afraid it is, sweetheart."

"But you told me you'd been divorced for two years!"

Noah inched a brow upward as her voice took on a shrewish tone he'd never heard from her before. But then, in all the time he'd known her, he'd never seen her upset before, either, he realized with a start. Suddenly he wondered if his placid little bride was everything she appeared to be.

"Sirena got a Mexican divorce and she just learned that it wasn't legal. She gave me copies of the divorce papers she's filed and says it should be final within a month. She also asked me to offer you her sincere apologies for what's happened."

"Sincere apologies?" Cynthia repeated, her voice climbing up another octave. "She destroyed my wedding day, and she offers her *sincere* apologies!"

"Cynthia, just calm down."

"Calm down!" she yelled at him. "How can I calm down when I don't know what to say to that chapel full of people waiting to see me get married? How could anything so scandalous happen to me?"

Noah touched her arm in a soothing gesture and frowned when she jerked away from his touch. His temper began to stir, but he kept it in check. After all, Cynthia had a right to be angry, he told himself. As she said, Sirena had just destroyed her wedding day.

"We'll go inside and tell our guests the truth," Noah said patiently. Though he knew it was inappropriate, his lips began to twitch as he saw a bit of humor in the entire mess. "This could be worse. She could have arrived too late to stop the wedding and you'd have found yourself married to a bigamist. Now *that* would be scandalous."

"Don't you dare laugh at me, Noah Samson!" she bellowed.

"I'm not laughing at you, Cynthia." His temper was beginning to stir again. "I'm simply trying to make you see that this is not the end of the world. Why, by this time next year, we'll be laughing about it, and just think of the story we'll be able to tell our grandchildren."

To Noah's surprise, his words didn't calm her, but only made her more furious, and he watched her fair skin become mottled and her eyes widen to the point that she looked bug-eyed. There was nothing pretty about an angry Cynthia, and Noah couldn't stop his mind from providing him with an image of Sirena, who looked magnificent when she was in a rage.

"I can't believe you would even say something like that," she spat at him. "I will never find this situation funny and I would certainly never repeat it to anyone, particularly my grandchildren. In fact, I'm not sure I want to marry you after what's happened," she stated petulantly. "And if you expect me to do so, you're going to have to prove to me that you're worth it."

"I see," Noah said as he narrowed his eyes and gazed down at her, allowing his temper full rein. His voice was no more than a whisper as he asked, "And how am I supposed to go about proving myself?"

Cynthia must have realized that she'd pushed him too far, because she took a couple of quick steps backward. "I . . . I don't know."

"Well, when you do, give me a call," he said as he unbuttoned his tuxedo jacket, shrugged out of it and tossed it over his shoulder, letting it dangle from one long finger. "After you've laid out the conditions, I'll tell you if I'm interested." He turned and started walking toward his car.

"Noah, where are you going?" Cynthia asked in alarm.

"Home," he answered without looking back.

"But what am I supposed to tell that chapel full of people?"

He stopped, glanced over his shoulder at her and, blessing Margaret Mitchell, said in his best Rhett Butler imitation, "Frankly, Cynthia, I don't give a damn what you tell them."

SIRENA GROANED and sat down at the side of the road in an unladylike sprawl. Her ankle was swelling and would soon be the size of an orange. Her skinned knees burned, her head ached, and she still smelled like chickens.

She'd walked in the direction the farmer had headed, figuring he must live nearby, but so far she hadn't even spotted a cow, let alone a farmhouse. Why in the world would Noah and his bride decide to get married out in the middle of nowhere?

She sighed, pushed herself to her feet and continued limping down the road, still surprised that Noah hadn't tried to kill her. She had the infamous redhead temper, but Noah's temper made hers pale in comparison.

However, thinking he would actually harm her was being melodramatic, she acknowledged. She'd seen him in many a rage during those three weeks they'd lived together, but she'd never been afraid of him. She'd always felt as if Noah would cut off his arm before he'd ever strike her in anger, and strangely she experienced a sensual quiver of longing in the pit of her stomach.

"Silly girl," she scolded herself. "What you had with him was pure and simple sex. Nothing more and nothing less."

But damn, it had been good in that way between them. No one, not even Jonathan, who appeared to be her perfect mate, had been able to make her body tremble and her mind go numb with nothing more than a look or a touch.

However, a marriage wasn't built on lust, she told herself firmly. It was built on compatibility, understanding and respect. It was built on reliance and teamwork, two concepts completely foreign to Noah the Dictator, who came from that old bastion that believed a man owned his wife until the day he died.

Sirena was so lost in her thoughts that she didn't hear the car until it was almost on top of her. She gaped in disbelief when it came to a stop and Noah leaned across the passenger seat, popped open the door of the low-slung red sports car and said, "Want a lift?"

She could only continue to stare at him. He looked like a modern-day pirate. His hair was windblown from the open windows. His ruffled shirt was unbuttoned to his waist, and the sight of his hair-covered chest caused her heart to do a crazy little jig in her chest.

"I, uh, don't think so," she replied as she regarded him cautiously, wondering why he was here instead of at the chapel consoling his disappointed bride. Was he going to murder her after all? But his expression was almost friendly. "I smell like chickens, and you may end up having to junk the car if you give me a ride."

He gave a negligent shrug of his shoulders. "I can afford to junk it if I can't get the smell out."

She arched a brow at that comment. One of their last arguments had been over money—the fact that she had more than she could ever spend in a lifetime and he wouldn't accept one blasted penny of it to help him get his fledgling computer firm off the ground.

Noah must have read her mind, because he said, "I told you I'd make it, Sirena."

"I never doubted you would," she replied defensively, though he hadn't made the statement as an accusation. "I just couldn't understand why you had to do it the hard way."

Noah didn't bother to respond, and he found himself really looking at her for the first time. Before, he'd been too angry to pay much attention to the changes two years had made, but now he took a detailed inventory of each and every one of them and he liked what he saw.

Sirena would never be called beautiful, he decided, but she'd never enter a room that every man in it didn't turn to look at her. Even dirty, banged-up and smelling like chickens, she was exotic. Her red hair gave her the look of a siren or, as he'd come to think of her, an enticing mermaid. Her huge brown eyes declared that she belonged between the sheets with a man between her thighs. Her nose was a bit too long, but its length was softened by a smattering of freckles. And her lips . . . well, Cupid's bow should be so perfect in symmetry.

His gaze flowed down her. She was tall for a woman, five feet nine inches. Her body was slim, almost boyish, but it was the way she moved that heated a man's blood. Unconsciously, she declared herself to be fire and dared any man to be brave enough to try to douse the flame.

Noah felt his body harden and realized that, fool that he was, he was beginning to fall beneath her spell again. But he'd gladly be a fool a hundred times over if he could relive those three glorious weeks of passion he'd spent with her. He raised his eyes to her face again and knew that that was exactly what he was going to do. Only this time he wouldn't let Sirena disappear until he was damn good and ready to let her go.

"Get in the car, Sirena."

He'd given the order in that familiar half demanding, half seductive tone of voice that had usually started one battle royal between them and ended with them in bed. Sirena took a nervous step backward and shook her head. She didn't know if she was denying his order or the fact that suddenly every part of her body was vibrating with desire, and that scared the hell out of her.

She spun away from the car and started walking down the side of the road, knowing she had to get away from him. However, she didn't get three feet before her injured ankle gave out and she found herself once again becoming intimately acquainted with the ground.

But that acquaintance was cut short when Noah arrived and scooped her up into his arms, making her feel as petite and fragile as his beautiful blond bride. For some reason, that feeling was the final straw to this nightmarish day, and to Sirena's utter horror, she did the most un-Barrington-like thing. She promptly burst into tears.

2

NOAH WAS BOTH SHOCKED and oddly touched by Sirena's tears. During their brief time together, he'd never seen her cry, and had in fact decided that Sirena's blue-blood heritage had bred out the capacity to succumb to anything as plebeian as tears.

He couldn't stop himself from pressing her head against his shoulder and dropping a soothing kiss against her brow as she sobbed like a bereft child. Unlike her fits of temper, however, her crying storm was over almost as quickly as it had begun. She was down to hiccups and sniffs by the time he reached the car and set her on the hood.

He knelt on one knee in front of her and began to gently palpate her swollen ankle. He carefully moved her foot up and down and rotated it from side to side, watching her face for any sign of undue pain. He was convinced the ankle wasn't broken when she didn't do anything more than give a small grimace.

Still cradling her ankle in one hand, he ran the other up her calf, stopping behind her abraded knee. His body went instantly hard again as he felt her tremble and knew that her involuntary response had nothing to do with her injury.

She whispered no from between her lips, and Noah understood that she was trying to deny the passion he could see flickering in her eyes. To his satisfaction, he could also see that she was losing the battle.

"Come on, mermaid," he said as he stood, scooped her back up into his arms and placed her in the car. "Let's go get you cleaned up and some ice on that ankle before it's as big as a basketball."

His use of the endearment struck stark terror into Sirena, because it caused that simmering passion that had awakened to proceed toward a full boil. Every ounce of common sense told her she had to make another break for it, but before she could convince her body to move, Noah had slammed the door, rounded the car and climbed in beside her.

Sirena purposely stared straight ahead, knowing that watching the play of muscle beneath his clothes as he maneuvered the car would be the beginning of her complete downfall. She also blessed the smell of chickens, which wiped out the pleasant scent of man and soap that had assaulted her when Noah held her in his arms.

An uncomfortable silence stretched between them as the sports car began to eat up the miles, and Sirena frowned when Noah slowed the car and turned onto a side road that looked even more poorly maintained than the one they were on. She parted her lips to ask him where they were going, but closed them abruptly, deciding that this was either the way to the nearest town or a shortcut, and she didn't want to pave the way for conversation between them by asking a silly question.

Several minutes passed with still no sign of civilization. Sirena was becoming more agitated by the minute. Why couldn't Noah live in Bedford, where she'd met him? At least there she'd be in familiar territory. But Noah had only been filling in at the blacksmith shop for his grandfather, who'd been recovering from an ailing gall bladder.

She let out a sigh of relief when she saw a public telephone standing alongside the road. It appeared that Ma

Bell could still come to the rescue when she was needed, even if it was in the boondocks.

"You can drop me off at that phone booth," she told Noah, her voice husky from tension. "If you'll tell me where I am, I'll call the rental car company and have them pick me up there. Then you can get back to your bride. I'm sure she's devastated and needs all the comfort you can give her."

Noah didn't respond until he pulled to a stop beside the phone booth. Then he said, "You need to stay off that ankle. Give me the number and I'll call the company."

Sirena wanted to object, but one quick glance at Noah's face told her he was determined. The last thing she wanted was an argument with him, so she obediently handed over the number. When he asked where she'd left her dead automobile, she told him, even though she had no idea why he needed to know. After all, she'd be able to direct the people to it when they picked her up.

Again she refused to look at Noah as he climbed out and walked to the phone booth, despite the fact that she was longing for that simple pleasure. Instead she leaned her head back against the seat and closed her eyes, letting her exhaustion come to the surface.

She'd begun to doze, but her eyes flew open when the car started. "What are you doing?" she asked in confusion.

Noah reached over and patted her arm. "I've taken care of everything, Sirena. Just go back to sleep."

"But—"

"Shhh," he said and patted her arm again.

By this time Sirena was too tired to put up a fight. She went back to sleep and didn't awaken again until Noah was lifting her out of the car.

Her first instinct was to snuggle against his chest, but she was, thankfully, one of those people who are instantly awake with total recall when they open their eyes. She was forced to wrap one arm around his neck to steady herself, but was able to brace the other against his chest to keep as much distance between them as possible.

She frowned as she eyed the small log cabin they were approaching and warily asked, "Where are we?"

"At my cabin," Noah answered as he climbed the stairs, easily shifting her weight so he could unlock the door. A moment later they were inside, and as Noah kicked the door closed behind them, Sirena's gaze flew around the one-room cabin.

Suddenly she understood exactly why Noah had decided to get married out in the sticks. The table was romantically set, complete with white Irish linen, fine china and crystal, tapered candlesticks and a bottle of champagne chilling in an ornate ice bucket. The bed had been turned down to reveal white satin sheets that were sprinkled with white rose petals.

Sirena was assaulted by two emotions at once. Embarrassment upon realizing that this was supposed to have been the newlyweds' honeymoon hideaway, and jealousy at the fact that all the white indicated that Noah's bride to be was quite innocent and he'd been very eager to remedy that fact.

She knew her cheeks had flamed crimson and she pointedly refrained from looking at the bed or Noah. She stared at the ice bucket and said, "I'm sorry I've caused you so much trouble, Noah, but at least you'll be able to take advantage of all this in another few weeks."

His response was a curt laugh. When she looked at him questioningly he gave her a rueful smile. "Cynthia's decided she doesn't want to marry me."

"Oh, Noah!" Sirena exclaimed in sincere distress. "Now I feel awful, but I'm sure that when she's had some time to calm down she'll change her mind."

"Maybe," Noah answered as he carried her toward a door on the far wall. He opened it to reveal a small bathroom and set her down on the toilet. "But I'm not sure I will."

"What does that mean?" Sirena asked as she watched him remove towels from a tiny linen closet.

He glanced over his shoulder at her and grinned. "I discovered this afternoon that my beautiful, obedient wife to be is just as shrewish and disobedient as my ex-wife to be."

Sirena supposed she should take offense at his words, but he'd delivered them so good-naturedly that she couldn't. Besides, she was experiencing a strange feeling of relief that his marriage had been called off, though for the life of her, she didn't know why.

"It sounds to me as if you should have taken more time to look beyond the rose blossom to see if there were any thorns," she told him.

"Sounds like it," he said agreeably. He laid fresh towels and a washcloth on the small wicker stand next to the old-fashioned, claw-footed tub, as well as a bottle of shampoo and a bar of soap. "Do you need any help getting into the tub?" he asked casually as he turned on the water.

"I can manage," Sirena answered, her cheeks once again flaming at the thought of Noah helping her climb into the bathtub. She knew she was being silly. The last person in the world she should be shy around was Noah. He knew her body more intimately than her doctor, and her doctor had delivered her!

She was sure Noah was thinking the same thought when his lips curved into his satyr's grin. But instead of taunting her, he said, "Let me get you something to change into. Then when you get undressed, throw your clothes out the door. I'll rinse them out and hang them up to dry."

"I can do that," she objected.

He gave a firm shake of his head. "You're going to get off that ankle and stay off it." He walked out before she could answer, and Sirena decided that he was just as dictatorial as ever.

When he returned, he hung a man-size, pale yellow shirt on a hook on the back of the door, saying, "You can change into this." He walked out again, closing the door after him before she even had a chance to thank him.

Sirena regarded the sheer cotton shirt, certain that it was virtually see-through, but gave a dismissive shrug. After all, she'd be wearing her underwear.

She rose to her feet awkwardly, noting with chagrin that her ankle was getting larger and more painful by the minute. She removed her simple shirtwaist dress and slip, and peeled off her ruined panty hose, tossing them into the wastebasket beside the sink. Then she threw her clothes out the bathroom door.

She'd no more than closed it when Noah said, "Where are the rest of your clothes, Sirena?"

"The rest?" she repeated uncertainly.

"Are you saying you were completely naked beneath this sedate little dress and prim and proper slip?"

"Of course not!" she exclaimed impatiently.

"Hand the rest over," he ordered.

"I will not."

His sigh was eloquent. "What's the matter, Sirena? Are you afraid of me?"

"Of course not!" she repeated, but even to her the words sounded too ardent.

"Then give me those lacy little nothings you wear so I can rinse them out. You know as well as I do that you can't stand to slip into used underwear after a bath."

Her eyes immediately focused on the shirt, and she once again confirmed that it was far too thin for convention's sake. But there was a challenge in Noah's voice telling her that even if she won the battle of keeping her underwear, she'd be losing the war, because the petty despot expected her to do just that.

Her temper flared as she stripped off her bra and panties, cracked open the door and tossed them out with the finesse of a stripper. His victorious chuckle told her that he'd used reverse psychology to get her to do exactly what he wanted, and her temper went on a rampage.

She'd fix that son of a blacksmith, she decided as she climbed into the tub and began to scrub her body. She was no longer a virginal twenty-four-year-old innocent, but a twenty-six-year-old woman who knew how to play the game as well as he did. He might still turn her on, but she was adult enough to handle it, and by the time her ride arrived, she'd have Noah Samson so hot to trot that he'd have to spend the next week under a cold shower.

That old saying, "Don't get mad, get even," had never sounded so right before, and Sirena actually began to hum to herself, ignoring the fact that it sounded like caterwauling to even her tone-deaf ears.

Noah smiled in triumph as he listened to Sirena's awful humming while he changed into low-riding denims and nothing more. Then he stuffed their clothes into a paper bag and carried it out to the car.

He dropped the bag into the trunk, slammed it shut and walked into the woods to hide his keys, knowing that if the vixen got her hands on them she'd be gone before he could blink. There wasn't a living soul within a twenty-mile radius of the cabin, and with her sprained ankle, Sirena had no chance of escape.

As he walked back to the cabin, he felt a pinprick of guilt about kidnapping her, but it quickly disappeared when he reminded himself how she'd so cavalierly up and left him two years ago. He was sensible enough to accept that all they'd had between them was passion and their breakup had been inevitable, but fate had just given him a chance to relive those three weeks that he'd remember for the rest of his life, and he was not about to turn his back on fate.

Inside the cabin, Noah removed the tray of lasagna from the refrigerator and slid it into the oven. By the time he uncorked the bottle of champagne and put the filled salad bowls on the table, he heard the water begin to drain from the bathtub. He took note of the hour and decided that everything was on schedule. By the time he took care of Sirena's ankle, dinner would be ready.

Sirena carefully dried herself. Once she was convinced that every drop of moisture had been removed from her body, she helped herself to the Shalimar bath powder sitting on the bathroom counter. Then she slid into Noah's shirt and buttoned it.

All her life, she'd wanted to be one of those exquisitely tiny women whom a man's shirt would engulf, but her wishes had been for naught. Though she was slim, she was also tall, and the shirttail didn't even reach mid-thigh. In fact, it barely fell far enough down her body to give her decent coverage, and she only had to roll the shirt cuffs twice to get them past her wrists.

But as she stared into the mirror, turned on the blow dryer and began to contemplate her revenge, she gave thanks for who and what she was. The roseate peaks of her breasts were hazily defined beneath the cotton, and the red curls that protected her femininity were definitely hinted at. She was positive that Noah hadn't realized just how sheer the shirt was, and she was going to make him rue the moment that he'd decided to make such a stupid power play over her underwear.

"Noah?" she called in her best damsel-in-distress voice as she opened the door.

He was instantly at her side, and Sirena wondered if she'd accurately assessed the rules of this game. The sight of him barefoot and bare-chested took her breath away. As he once again scooped her into his arms and her palm came into contact with the crisp dark hair on his chest, she knew the odds were against her. But there hadn't ever been a Barrington woman who'd lost in the battle between the sexes, and she wasn't about to become the first, she vowed.

Noah carried her to the small sofa in front of the fireplace, where a low-burning fire cheerfully flared, and settled her against the cushions. Without a word, he disappeared into the bathroom and then reappeared with a first-aid kit. He knelt in front of her, lifted her foot and rested it on his knee, where he proceeded to wrap her ankle with an Ace bandage.

When that was done, he opened a tube of antiseptic cream, smoothed it onto her abused knees and then settled her foot on a nearby hassock. As he plopped a plastic bag of ice cubes on her ankle, he announced, "Dinner will be ready in about five minutes."

He crossed to the stove, and Sirena frowned at his muscular back. The fool hadn't even bothered to look at the shirt that revealed every feminine asset she had! Was he blind or simply doltish?

She knew it wasn't the former, so she decided it was the latter and folded her arms over her chest as she glared at the small fire in front of her. She told herself that all those little tingles that had crept over her skin the entire time he was caring for her wounds had *not* been desire.

Since it was late June, the fire hadn't been lit for heat but for effect, and Sirena soon found herself uncomfortably warm in front of it. She glanced around the room for a retreat, but quickly realized that her only comfortable option was that rose petal-covered bed, and she wouldn't have touched it with a ten-foot pole if she'd been offered a million dollars to do so.

"Did the rental car company say when they'd be here to pick me up?" she asked.

Noah was concentrating on the food he'd just removed from the oven and he shook his head. He carried the tray to the table and poured champagne into the waiting glasses. Then he walked to the sofa, handed Sirena the ice cube bag and carried her to the table. After placing her on a chair, he propped her foot on another one and put the ice back on her ankle. He sat down at the opposite end of the small table and smiled.

"I don't know about you, but I'm starving. Eat up," he ordered, digging into the lasagna, still seemingly unaware of her provocative attire.

Though Sirena would have given anything to be able to turn her nose up at the food, the fact was, she was starving, and she attacked the pasta with relish. Even the champagne hit the spot, and she didn't object when Noah refilled her glass. By the time she finished eating, she felt replete and leaned back with a contented sigh.

With a wry smile at Noah, she lifted her champagne glass toward him in a salute, saying, "To the best of times, and to the worst of times."

Noah chuckled, clinked his glass against hers and asked, "And into which category do I fall in your life?"

Sirena met his indigo gaze, which was far too warm for her peace of mind. She glanced quickly away and said, "Both, I suppose."

He sipped from his glass, peering over its rim at her as he raised his foot and placed it beside hers on the chair between them. His bare toes brushed hers, sending her pulse into overdrive.

"Why did you leave me like that, Sirena?" he asked. "Didn't you know how much it would hurt me?"

Sirena could only shake her head as inexplicable tears welled into her eyes. During that last argument, he'd told her to pack her bags and get out, and though it had hurt like hell, for the first time in those three weeks she'd obeyed him without question.

"You told me to leave, Noah."

"I was angry."

"So was I, and that was the problem. It seemed that we were perpetually angry with each other, and I couldn't see a future in that. You couldn't accept me for what I was, and I couldn't accept you for what you were. Divorce was the only sensible answer."

"You didn't give us enough time to look for a sensible compromise."

"Oh, come on, Noah," she muttered in disbelief. "You didn't want a compromise. You wanted complete control."

"I wasn't trying to control you, Sirena. I was only attempting to be a good husband."

"Telling me how to dress was being a good husband?"

He scowled at her. "I didn't want other men lusting after my wife."

"Noah, you make me sound as if I were some kind of...of femme fatale. My word, I was a twenty-four-year-old virgin. Don't you think that if I'd had so many men lusting after me, I would have lost my halo long before I met you?"

"Your appeal is so unconscious that you don't even realize it's there," he defended.

Sirena shook her head again, but decided it wasn't worth arguing over. "What about the fact that you absolutely refused to let me go home to get my affairs in order?"

"I didn't refuse. I told you it would have to wait until I could go with you."

"But you wouldn't even give me a possible date, because you were too busy struggling to get your business off the ground. Then when I offered you the money to get you on your feet so you wouldn't have to work yourself to death, you turned your nose up at it."

"A man does not live off his wife, Sirena."

She slammed her open palm down on the table. "And that was just what was wrong with our entire relationship! You were so caught up in the archaic past that you couldn't see past the end of your chauvinistic nose."

Noah glared down at the liquid in his glass. "So you hated me for what I was. For what I was brought up to be."

"No!" Sirena's hand shot involuntarily across the table to capture his at the hurt tone of his voice. "I never hated you, I simply didn't understand you. You were a man of the past, while I was a woman of the future. I couldn't be what you wanted me to be any more than you could be what I wanted you to be."

He raised his eyes to hers, and his gaze was so intense that it seared through her. "There were times when we were both exactly what the other wanted us to be."

Her fingers curled around his in an angry grip. "And that's all we had in common, Noah. Plain old sex."

"No," he said with a firm shake of his head. "What we shared could never be defined as plain old sex. It was much more than that."

"That may be true." She released his hand and let out a weary sigh. "All I know is that when you took me to bed, I was the most satisfied woman in the world. But when I climbed out of it, I was the most dissatisfied woman in the world."

She didn't know what she'd expected his response to be to her confession, but it certainly wasn't that he'd simply rise to his feet and begin to clear the table. When the chore was done, he carried her back to the sofa and returned to the sink to wash the dishes.

The fire had almost died, but Sirena was still hot, particularly when she cast a few surreptitious glances toward Noah's muscular back. Unwanted memories stirred as she recalled the feel of that back, so soft, yet so hard, and when her fingers began to itch to touch him, she gripped them together tightly in her lap.

It didn't help, because now that the sensual memories had managed to creep in, they wouldn't go away, and she shifted restlessly on the sofa, wishing that her ride would get here. She no longer wanted to wage war against Noah. She was quite willing to declare him the victor and just go home where she led a peaceful and quiet life.

She jumped when Noah suddenly appeared in front of her, the empty champagne glasses in his hand and the half-full bottle tucked beneath his arm. He sat down beside her, handed her the glasses and filled them. After he set the bottle on the floor at his feet, he took one of the glasses from her and leaned back against the cushions with a weary sigh.

Sirena gulped half the wine as he spread his knees apart and his thigh came to rest against hers, sending shock waves of pleasure shooting through her. She would have scooted away from his touch, but she was already squeezed into the corner against the arm of the sofa and there was no place to go but up. She knew what interpretation Noah would put on that, and even if he was correct, she wasn't about to let him know it.

"How's the ankle?" he asked, closing his eyes.

"Better," she managed to answer around the lump in her throat.

He nodded and didn't say anything more. The silence in the room became so palpable that when the mantel clock began to chime the hour, Sirena let out a gasp of surprise and spilled the remainder of her champagne down the front of her shirt.

Noah opened his eyes and smiled as he followed the trail of champagne that had molded the shirt to one breast. He leaned forward, lifted the champagne bottle and refilled her glass. As he placed the bottle back on the floor, he said, "Keeping yourself in clean clothes must be a full-time job."

Sirena knew he was trying to get a rise out of her and refused to take the bait. Instead she said, "Speaking of clothes, mine should be dry by now. I'd better get changed, because my ride should be arriving soon."

He resumed his relaxed position against the cushions and closed his eyes again. "You have plenty of time."

He sounded so sure that Sirena regarded him suspiciously. She wanted to ask him just how much time she did have, but she knew he was waiting for her to do so. She was just contrary enough not to give him that satisfaction.

The silence continued for another fifteen minutes before Noah broke it by asking, "So what has the poor little rich girl been doing to keep herself occupied for the past two years?"

Sirena automatically bristled at his poor-little-rich-girl routine. During that time of heaven and hell they'd spent together, he'd often used those words, and they had never been spoken in a complimentary manner.

She glanced toward him angrily and discovered that he was watching her, grinning devilishly as he waited for the inevitable explosion. He was baiting her again, she realized, and she forced herself to control her temper.

She gave a bored shrug of her shoulders. "Not taking cooking or housecleaning lessons, that's for sure," she responded, remembering how horrified he'd been to learn that his new wife couldn't boil water and had needed an instruction manual to use a broom.

To her surprise, he burst into hearty laughter. Then he caught her hand and brought it to his lips, pressing a quick kiss against her knuckles. "I was a bastard at times, wasn't I?"

"Yes," Sirena answered, not about to give him an inch and wondering how she could remove her hand from his without letting him know the effect his touch was having on her. "But I suppose you were entitled. There were times when I wasn't very nice myself."

He put her hand back in her lap and gave it a comforting pat. "True. So, tell me what you've been doing."

"Things," she said vaguely, finding herself unwilling to share her triumphs with him, and not quite certain why. She supposed it was because he'd often accused her of having no purpose in life, and she'd be the first to admit that at that time she'd been drifting.

But through his eyes, she'd seen just how shallow her existence was, and when she left him, she'd decided to change that by starting the Barrington Foundation. She still couldn't wield a broom with skill, but she'd proved herself to be one hell of an administrator.

Noah watched the expressions flitting across her face as she became lost in her thoughts, and her withdrawal from him made him unreasonably angry. She was shutting him out, just as she'd constantly shut him out two years ago. It was as frustrating now as it had been then; it was one of the reasons why he'd constantly pushed her into a fight. Battling with her had also helped him cope with his feeling of impotence whenever he remembered just who and what she was.

It was only after they were married that he learned Sirena was not only wealthy, but so filthy rich that the federal government could have come to her for a loan. All he'd had to offer her was an efficiency apartment filled with rented furniture, and if he'd pooled his assets, they probably wouldn't have amounted to five hundred bucks. He'd lived in mortal fear of the day when she'd discover that the novelty of him had worn off and walk out, which was another reason why he'd goaded her at every opportunity. He'd thought that the sooner she left, the less it would hurt; but he'd been wrong, and that admission only made him more angry.

"Noah, when is my ride supposed to be here?" Sirena asked, choosing that inopportune moment to interrupt his thoughts.

He rolled his head toward her, his anger still cresting, though he knew it was directed more at himself and his stupid insecurities than at her. "I'm your ride, Sirena, and we'll leave when I'm damn good and ready."

She blinked in surprise at his irritated tone of voice. "But you called the rental car company and told them to pick me up."

"I told them where they could pick up their car."

Sirena shook her head, unable—or maybe unwilling—to assimilate what he was saying. "I don't understand."

"Don't you?" he rasped as he caught her head in one large hand and drew her toward him. "You're my wife, and I've been without a woman for a very long time."

"No!" Sirena exclaimed. But what was she denying? The fact that she was his wife? The fact that he wanted her and she returned that need? She knew it would be fruitless to struggle against his superior strength, and she decided to use common sense as his mouth came dangerously closer. "Noah, we're getting a divorce."

"You're getting a divorce. You never asked me if I wanted one."

"But—"

Her objection was cut short as his lips sealed over hers, and he swallowed her groan of protest as he pulled her against him. She placed her hands against his bare chest to push him away, but that feeling of soft hardness melted away her resistance. With another groan, she burrowed against him.

"Ah, mermaid," he whispered in her ear as he tumbled her back onto the sofa. "I've missed you so much."

"It's only sex," she gasped as he rocked his hips against hers, showing her the effect she was having on him.

"You can call it whatever you want," he murmured huskily as his fingers went to work on the buttons of her shirt. "All I know is that it's damn good."

Oh, is he right about that, Sirena thought as he parted the fabric and his hands and lips began to honor her. He licked, kissed, nuzzled and kneaded until she thought she'd go insane, and she began to tear at the buttons on the front of his jeans, now frantic to feel every gorgeous naked inch of him against her heated flesh.

"Why don't you move into the twentieth century and buy a pair of pants with a zipper?" she asked hoarsely as her trembling fingers failed in their third attempt to release a button.

His chuckle was throaty, and his expression was one of pure male satisfaction as he seductively stroked himself against her hand. "Because then I wouldn't be able to experience the exquisite torture you put me through while you undo my buttons."

Sirena had to close her eyes and suck in a deep breath as his words thrummed through her with a devastating effect.

The air rushed out of her lungs as he pressed tiny kisses along her hairline, encouraging her with, "Come on, mermaid. Get the torture over with so we can move on to better things."

The words called up images so erotic that they snapped her back to reality. "Oh, heaven help me, I can't go through with this," she whispered regretfully. "It's wrong. It's so wrong."

"No, Sirena. It's right. It's so right that you have to go through with it." He took one of her hands and placed it against his racing heart. "Feel what you do to me here, and here," he said, transferring her hand to the front of his jeans. "And I do the same to you." He touched his hand against her heaving breast and then her melting femininity.

But Sirena shook her head, refusing to accept that truth. "Don't you see that it's so right that it has to be wrong? We make each other burn, and no matter how many times we try to put out the fire, we fail. This passion we share is insatiable, Noah. If we give in to it again it's going to destroy us."

Noah frowned as he watched tears flood her eyes, and a wave of tenderness flowed through him. He tangled his fingers in her hair and brushed his thumbs across her high cheekbones, loving the feel of her velvet-soft skin and the silken caress of her magnificent mane of hair.

"What you say may be true, Sirena. The problem is, if I don't give in to it again I'm going to be destroyed."

Sirena parted her lips to object, but Noah laid a finger against them to stop her from speaking. "You walked out on me before I was ready to let you go. I've been given a chance to remedy that situation, and I have to take advantage of it. I can never be whole until I complete this chapter of my life, and even though I'm sure you'll deny it, it's true for you, too, or you wouldn't be responding to me like this."

He drew in a deep breath before reluctantly concluding with, "You're still my wife, Sirena. Since you are, I want another three weeks with you and I'm going to have them."

The man was crazy, Sirena decided as she felt herself grow pale at his announcement. Absolutely certifiable, committable, crazy!

She gave him a frantic shove, but he didn't budge an inch. Before she could try again, he rose to his feet and walked into the bathroom. The moment he shut the door behind him, Sirena was on her feet and out the front door of the cabin, moving swiftly in spite of her sprained ankle.

3

WHEN SIRENA'S FEET touched the ground, she knew she was in trouble. Her shoes were still in the bathroom, and there was no way she could make it down the gravel road or through the thick woods without them.

That left Noah's car. He had the keys, but this poor little rich girl had a few tricks up her sleeve that Noah didn't know about. During her early teenage years one of her best friends was a larcenous little urchin who, much to the chauffeur's chagrin, had taught Sirena how to hot-wire a car.

She'd just finished buttoning her shirt when she reached his car, only to discover that the doors were locked. She looked around for an object large enough to smash a window, but it seemed even Mother Nature was in cahoots with Noah. The largest boulder she could find was the size of a pea.

She wanted to scream and curse and throw things, but she knew that all she'd gain from it would be a release of tension. What she needed was a plan, and the only one she could come up with was to go back inside, bash Noah over the head and then either find his keys or a way to break into his sporty red racer.

The thought of physical violence, even toward a man as deserving of it as Noah, made her nauseated. But her only other option was to sleep with him to get what she wanted, and there was no way she was going to do that.

She jumped in surprise when Noah drawled from directly behind her, "I hid the keys and the distributor cap in the woods. There's no escape, Sirena."

"Then I'll walk out!" she yelled as she spun around to face him.

His smile was maddeningly calm. "There isn't a living soul within a twenty-mile radius of here. You would never make it on that ankle, let alone in those skimpy little sandals that you called shoes."

"What do you mean *called* shoes?" she asked suspiciously.

Noah arched a brow. "You mean I didn't mention that? I just sent your sandals off to join your clothes. I tossed them into the fireplace," he lied, knowing perfectly well that her sandals were tucked into a dark corner beneath the bed with his own shoes.

"You burned my clothes! How dare you?"

He gave a nonchalant shrug. "If it'll make you feel any better, my clothes went up with yours. All we have in the house is the shirt you're wearing and my trousers, although I'd gladly dispose of either of them at your command."

His gaze swept her body in a bold appraisal that made Sirena's blood boil. The worst part was, not all of that boil could be attributed to anger, and that made her furious.

"You're insane, Noah. Absolutely, positively, no-questions-asked insane, and what you're doing is called kidnapping. If you don't take me to the nearest town this very instant, I'll make sure that you not only land in the clink, but that they throw away the key."

He widened his eyes innocently. "Taking one's wife on a belated honeymoon isn't called kidnapping, Sirena. It's called romanticism."

"Not when said wife has not only filed for divorce, but is taken away against her will," she countered, perching her hands on her hips and glaring at him. "Besides, there are going to be people looking for me. I'm no longer the fluff-headed little ingenue you married two years ago. I'm a woman with a great many responsibilities, and when I don't show up to take care of them, the alarm will be sounded."

Noah leaned against the car and grinned at her. "I took care of that, too. After I called the rental car agency, I called your cousin Maggie. I told her that you and I had decided to spend a few weeks together to see if we could reconcile before it was too late. She was quite willing to make up a story to soothe everyone until you came back. She decided that that way you won't have to face embarrassing questions if it doesn't work out.

"By the way," he continued as he reached out to tug playfully on a lock of her hair, his grin widening when Sirena slapped his hand away, "Maggie wished us luck. She and I have run into each other a few times over the years, and she's always been quite supportive of me. It seems that the Barrington women never get divorced, and the entire family has been appalled at having to try to live down your scandal."

Sirena's mouth opened and closed several times during his dissertation, but she simply couldn't find words terrible enough to fling at him. She decided that the first thing she'd do when she got out of this mess was beef up the Barrington family's list of official swear words.

"I am not staying here, Noah."

"Not only are you staying, but you're getting off that ankle and staying off it until I say you can get up."

With that he leaned over, hefted Sirena over his shoulder like a sack of potatoes and carried her kicking and screaming back into the house, where he dumped her inelegantly onto the sofa.

"You're going to pay for this, Noah Samson," she vowed as she scrambled into a sitting position and readjusted her shirttail, which had climbed so far up her body that if Noah hadn't seen everything God gave her, it was only because he hadn't been looking.

"I'm sure I will," he answered, his grin firmly in place, the hot glow in his eyes informing her that he had indeed been looking. "I'll just have to make sure that I get my punishment's worth."

His words made Sirena's temper flag and every drop of color drain from her face. "I won't sleep with you," she said quietly, but insistently. "If you want me, you'll have to rape me."

His grin faded and his eyes grew so cold that Sirena shivered. "Well, you know what they say, '*Que será será.*'" Without missing a beat, he said, "I'm going out for some fresh air. When I get back, I expect to see that ankle up with ice on it. If it isn't, I may have to do what I should have done two years ago, and that's turn you over my knee."

When he walked out the door and slammed it behind him, Sirena couldn't decide if she was furious or terrified. Without even realizing what she was doing she immediately put her foot on the hassock and dropped the ice bag over her ankle. Then she leaned back and tried to figure out what her options were.

In less than five minutes, she realized that she had none. Noah had thought of everything. He'd said that he'd hidden both his keys and the distributor cap, so even if she could break into the car, it wouldn't do her any good. He'd destroyed her clothes and shoes, so she couldn't hide out in the woods to escape him.

Tears welled into her eyes as she accepted the hopelessness of her situation, but she refused to let herself succumb to a much-needed crying jag. She had to remain calm and use her wits to convince Noah to take her out of here. But what kind of argument would work on a man who'd just stated that he would resort to rape if he had to?

Though she shuddered at the thought, her mind refused to accept his threat. Noah was an infuriating tyrant, but he was not violent. He would never take her against her will. At least he wouldn't have two years ago, but look how much *she*'d changed since then, and she had no idea what changes had taken place inside Noah.

By this time, the entire situation had become far too complicated, and Sirena rested her head against the back of the sofa, doing what she always did in times of great stress. She went to sleep.

NOAH SAT ON THE TOP STEP of the cabin and stared at nothing in particular. He was frustrated, angry and completely disgusted with himself. He couldn't believe that he'd just told Sirena he would rape her. What had started out as an impulsive game was now turning into something serious and disturbing, and he didn't like one thing about it. He raked both hands through his hair, trying to analyze his motivation. As he began to understand it, he became even more upset with himself.

From the moment he'd laid eyes on Sirena two years ago, he'd wanted her. When he'd had her and discovered that he was the first, he'd felt possessive. The thought that someone else would experience what he'd found in her arms had made him jealous, and that jealousy had made him push her into marriage.

What had been between them was nothing more than undiluted passion, but he'd wanted more from her. He'd wanted to know her every thought and feeling. He'd needed to know that he was the first thing she wanted to see when she opened her eyes in the morning and the last thing when she closed them at night. He'd wanted to succeed for her, so that she would brag about what a wonderful man he was and believe every blessed word of it.

Then he'd learned how rich she was, and he'd realized that no matter what he achieved, Sirena Angelica Barrington would never need him. That had scared the hell out of him.

He cursed as he rose from the stairs, paced to the car and leaned against it. Her money had made him insecure and still bothered him. The average man would now consider him rich, but hell, he probably didn't even fall into the first fifty thousand on Sirena's scale of who was who when it came to wealth. When he married her, the only thing he'd had to offer her was a good roll in the hay, and without anything but sex between them, he'd known he'd never be able to hold on to her. In defense he'd sent her away and ended up regretting it.

Now, he was regretting what he'd done today, and he knew he couldn't go through with his wild scheme. If he carried it out, she'd end up hating him, and he'd never be able to live with that.

SIRENA'S EYES SNAPPED open the moment she heard the door close. She regarded Noah warily as he walked to the sofa and dropped a large paper bag beside her.

"Your clothes are in there," he told her. "While you dig them out, I'll get your shoes."

"I thought you said you burned my clothes," she said, watching him kneel by the bed and remove her sandals and a pair of running shoes from beneath it.

"I lied." He sat down on the floor and leaned his back against the mattress.

Every ounce of Barrington common sense told Sirena to grab her clothes and run. Instead, she eyed him curiously. "Why?"

He chuckled as he tossed her shoes toward her, but the sound was mirthless. The sandals landed just inches from the hassock.

"Curiosity killed the cat, mermaid. Get yourself dressed and let's get the hell out of here."

Sirena frowned, sensing that Noah was deeply upset. For some inexplicable reason that made her deeply upset. "Noah, what's wrong?"

"Not a thing." He pushed himself to his feet. "I don't want you bouncing around on that ankle, so I'll wait outside until you're dressed. You have five minutes, Sirena, and then I'm coming in to get you."

He was gone before she could question him further, and her frown deepened as she slipped into her clothes, noting that though they hadn't been washed, the smell of chickens was beginning to fade.

She was sitting on the sofa, fully clothed and shod, when Noah returned seven, not five, minutes later. She'd been keeping track.

Without a word, he retrieved a formfitting navy-blue T-shirt from the paper bag and pulled it on. When he was done, Sirena started to stand, only to find herself swept off her feet and into his arms.

"Your ankle isn't that seriously injured, Sirena, but it will be if you don't take care of it. Promise me you'll stay off it for a few days and give it a rest."

His words were innocuous, but there was something so final in the tone of his voice that Sirena's heart lurched.

"I promise."

"There's hope for you yet, kid."

She had the choice of crying or nodding, so she nodded, because she didn't know why she wanted to cry.

Minutes later they were headed away from his mountain retreat, and though she tried to concentrate on all the twists and turns the car took, she knew she'd never be able to find her way back to the cabin. Before an hour had passed, Noah pulled into the Hagerstown, Maryland shuttle airport where she'd landed that morning.

He gripped the steering wheel and glanced toward her. "Are you going to make a scene if I carry you inside, or are you going to simply sit back and enjoy the ride?"

She wanted to reach out and smooth the crease lines on his brow. "It seems to me I promised to stay off my ankle."

He gave her the first honest smile he'd given her all day before he climbed out and rounded the car. Inside the terminal, he arranged for her ticket and then sat down beside her to wait.

The silence between them stretched until Sirena thought she'd go insane if she didn't engage in some conversation. Finally she said, "Tell me about Samson Software."

Noah glanced toward her with one brow arched. "It's not Samson Software any longer."

"Why not?" Sirena asked, taken by surprise. "You always said you'd never change the name because the company was your first child."

Noah's grin was rueful. "And a pretty little mermaid wrinkled her nose at the name and told me that it stank, because she couldn't think of one decent slogan to promote it."

Sirena blushed deeply as she admitted, "I said that because I was jealous, Noah. You spent more time with that business than with me."

Something changed in his expression, but Sirena couldn't put her finger on it. All she knew was that it made her heart heavy and her chest hurt.

"Noah . . ."

Her flight was announced.

"It's time for you to go, Sirena."

She nodded, needing to say something significant, but all that came out was "It's been . . ."

". . . nice," he finished for her as he helped her stand and guided her into the line leading through the security gate. "Take care of that ankle."

"I will," she said as the airline official opened her purse and checked through it, the terminal being too small to warrant an X-ray machine. "You take care of yourself."

"Always," Noah said.

The woman handed back Sirena's purse and urged her out the door to the macadam she had to cross to get to the small jet.

She limped her way up the stairs, but just before she climbed inside, she glanced back. Noah was watching her, his hands stuffed into his pockets. He pulled one out and waved at her and she waved back, her heart becoming even heavier.

Inside the aircraft, she chose a seat on the side away from the terminal so she wouldn't have to look at Noah. It was finally over, but it had hurt worse to walk away from him this time than it had two years ago.

It seemed like forever before the pilot started the engine and the plane began to move. Sirena sighed as they coasted forward, feeling as if she were leaving with everything hanging up in the air, which was utterly ridiculous, of course.

Then the pilot did the most horrible thing. He circled around and Sirena had a perfect view of the terminal. As they picked up speed and lifted into the air, she saw Noah framed in the window. She told herself it was only a trick of the light, but he looked as lonely as she felt.

NOAH GATHERED HIS MAIL and let himself into his condominium. He normally enjoyed the plush luxury and took a few moments to glance around, savoring it. But since the day Sirena had popped into and out of his life with the expertise of a jack-in-the-box, he hadn't been able to pay much attention to anything, let alone his surroundings.

As he listened to his messages on the answering machine, he began to sort through the letters, placing bills in one pile on the small table in the entryway and tossing junk mail into the wastepaper basket. His attention was drawn away from the chore as he heard Cynthia's simpering voice begging him to call her.

He wavered over the decision whether or not to return her call and decided against it. They'd talked half a dozen times since their disastrous wedding day, and the truth was Noah felt cornered and confused. He felt like an ogre, however, when he heard another message from her and it was evident she was crying. He was going to have to call her, he admitted resignedly, but he'd do it later.

He continued to sort through his mail while he listened to the remainder of his messages, but when he reached the letter in the middle of the stack, he heard nothing but the rapid beating of his heart. The return address read: Harcourt, Harcourt and Devereaux, Attorneys-at-Law.

Something inside Noah twisted in denial as he recognized the name of the law firm listed on the divorce papers Sirena had given him. It could only be the divorce decree, but she'd told him the divorce wouldn't be final for at least a month, and he wasn't prepared for it to be happening this soon.

Part of him insisted that he open the letter immediately. Another part urged him to wait. He decided to listen to the latter as he dropped the letter onto the stack of bills and finished looking at his mail. When he was done, he replayed his messages, jotting down information and numbers he needed. Then he walked onto the balcony and gazed out at the city lights.

As he rested his elbows on the railing, he analyzed his feelings. When Sirena divorced him the first time, it had devastated him, but he'd had his anger to give him a buffer to the pain. Now, without that anger, it hurt like hell, and he didn't know why. They'd been apart for two years. He'd accepted the inevitable. But as he'd told Sirena the other day, he felt as if he had an uncompleted chapter in his life, and Noah never left anything unfinished. At least he never had until now, because in this instance he hadn't been given a choice.

He also didn't know what to do about Cynthia. He'd courted her for a year, determined to ensure that he didn't make the same mistake of rushing into marriage that he'd made with Sirena. Yet when she lost her temper at the chapel, he'd realized that he didn't really know her. Was he in love with her, or simply in love with the life he'd planned on building with her?

He didn't have any answers. With a sigh, he walked back inside, dug the letter from Sirena's attorneys out of the stack of bills and ripped it open. But it wasn't a divorce decree. It was a document for him to sign releasing any claim he might have on Sirena's money.

Noah scowled. He'd never wanted a penny of her money, and while he knew that the form was simply a means for her attorneys to tie up any loose ends, it made him unreasonably angry.

His first urge was to crumple it and toss it into the wastepaper basket with the remainder of his junk mail. Instead, he dropped it onto the table beside the check Sirena had given him for Cynthia's parents to cover their wedding expenses, an act that he'd perform himself when the time came.

As he stared down at both pieces of paper, he couldn't decide which of them rankled more, because he considered both a backhanded slap in the face. One indicated he was a gigolo; the other said he wasn't capable of paying his own way. The poor little rich girl hadn't changed and never would, so why couldn't he get her off his mind?

With an irritated curse, he returned to the balcony and resumed his perusal of the city lights. When the phone rang and he listened to Cynthia leave still another message, he simply couldn't bring himself to talk to her. His past and his present were colliding, and he knew he had to resolve his feelings for both women before he could move forward.

What he needed was some time to think, he finally decided, and he walked into his bedroom and stuffed a duffel bag with several changes of clothing. He'd go back to the cabin until he could decide what he wanted to do.

"SIRENA, ARE YOU just now getting home?" asked Sirena's Aunt Tabitha, a scolding cluck in her voice as Sirena barreled in the front door. "You're going to be late for dinner and I specifically called the office and left a message that we were having a special guest tonight."

"Sorry, but something came up at the last minute," Sirena said, automatically dropping a peck on her aunt's plump cheek before heading up the stairs. "Tell Mother and Grandmother to start dinner without me. I should be down before you're through with the appetizers."

"But, Sirena . . ."

Sirena waved her aunt to silence. "Just tell them, Aunt Tabitha. Please?"

"All right, but they aren't going to like it."

"So what else is new?" Sirena muttered to herself as she rushed to her room.

She loved her family dearly, but they had a tendency to drive her crazy, and she felt that old familiar urge to pack her bags and run. However, she knew it would be fruitless. Before she ever made it to the front door, all three women would have her feeling so guilty that she'd end up slinking back to her room with the spinelessness of a worm.

Master guilt-making was another female Barrington trait, and Sirena had worked very hard over the years to make sure it wasn't one she cultivated. Unfortunately, by not learning it, she'd fallen too often into the trap of feeling guilty, and that irritated her.

If the guilt had been confined to her family, it wouldn't have been so bad, but it extended into every avenue of her life. A good example was her guilty feelings about Noah. All week long she'd been thinking about how lonely he looked as she flew away. She couldn't help feel it was because she'd made him lose his Cynthia. It was obvious he was madly in love with Cynthia. Why else would he have prepared such an elaborate honeymoon retreat for his new wife? Along with that thought came the strange pang of jealousy that she'd experienced every time she recalled walking into the chapel and seeing Noah at his beautiful bride's side.

Sirena scolded herself severely for behaving like a schoolgirl ninny, as she stripped off her dress, tossed it onto the bed and hurried into the bath. Noah the dictator was out of her life forever. She should be giving thanks, not mooning over him.

She showered and changed in record time. When she raced out of her room, she collided with Ben, the portly middle-aged butler, nearly sending them both sprawling.

"Are you all right, Miss Sirena?" Ben dropped the bags he was carrying and latched onto her arms to steady her.

"I'm fine," she assured him, her gaze dropping to the two suitcases at his feet. "We have a visitor?"

A peculiar little smile curved Ben's normally straight-as-a-board lips. "Yes, ma'am." Before Sirena could inquire who the visitor was, Ben said, "You'd better get a move on, Miss Sirena. Mrs. Mullen has already served the appetizer, and you know how your grandmother fusses when you're late for dinner."

"How well I know," she grumbled as she took off.

She was halfway down the stairs before it dawned on her that Ben had been carrying the suitcases into her wing of the house. As there was only one guest room and it shared her bath, that meant this surprise dinner guest/ visitor had to be an old school friend or a favorite cousin come to pay her a visit. She hurried toward the dining room, eager to discover who it was.

As she approached it, she heard feminine laughter in response to a low male voice, and she wondered which of her mother's or grandmother's swains was here tonight. Both widows had dated for years, but neither had any intention of marrying. They claimed that their husbands had been the loves of a lifetime, and that it wouldn't be fair to commit themselves to a man whom they could never consider more than second best.

Sirena stepped into the room, a welcoming smile on her face. But the smile died and her mouth dropped open in shock as her gaze landed on Noah, who was sitting at the head of the table in the honored master-of-the-house chair that had been vacant since her father's death. Not even her two brothers had been allowed to sit in it.

"Noah? What are you doing here?" she questioned in disbelief.

Noah's head snapped up and he blinked at the vision in the doorway. He'd never seen Sirena look as lovely as she did in the gauzy turquoise sundress, whose simple lines screamed class. Delicate white sandals adorned her feet and laced around her ankles in an intricate pattern that emphasized their slimness. Her hair, tumbling around her face and shoulders in fashionable disarray, made her look so sexy it took his breath away.

His heartbeat resounded in his ears and desire swept through him with such force that his wineglass trembled in his hand. Carefully, he set it on the table and rose to his feet, knowing that he had to get to Sirena before she regained her wits and blew everything.

He walked toward her purposefully, smiling his best seducer-of-the-year smile. "I know we agreed to tell your family about our attempt to reconcile together, darling, but I finished my business early and just couldn't wait to see you. Forgive me?"

"Wha—" Sirena began in horror, but her question was cut off as Noah snatched her into his arms and treated her to a kiss so potent she would have needed fog lights to find her way through the haze in her mind.

4

NOAH REALIZED he'd made a mistake in kissing Sirena, even if it had been his only option to shut her up. As her tongue stroked his and a soft little mew vibrated in the back of her throat, part of his body went weak while the other part went hard. He was about ready to go under for the third time when he heard Sirena's Aunt Tabitha exclaim, "Oh, how romantic!"

At the reminder that he and Sirena were definitely not alone he forced himself to pull away from the kiss. He didn't, however, release his hold on Sirena, who was leaning weakly against him. He glanced over his shoulder and watched the pleasantly plump Tabitha dab a lacy handkerchief at the corners of her eyes.

His gaze shifted to Sirena's grandmother and mother, both of whom looked like silver-haired queens. Their smiles indicated they were as touched as Sirena's aunt, though it was apparent that they'd never allow themselves to be as demonstrative about it.

"Please excuse us for a moment, ladies," he said as he wrapped a secure arm around Sirena's waist and began moving her limp body toward the dining room doorway. "I'm afraid Sirena's quite overcome by my sudden appearance and needs a breath of fresh air."

"Take your time," her grandmother, Ophelia Barrington, said with a knowing chuckle.

"Yes, take your time," her mother, Pamela, echoed, amusement dancing in her brown eyes. "In fact, we could always send a tray upstairs."

Noah felt Sirena stiffen at that one and knew he had to get her out of the room and fast. "That won't be necessary. We'll return shortly."

He hurried her toward the front door and was amazed when the butler miraculously appeared and opened it for them. Noah had never seen much use for servants, but right now he wondered if he shouldn't revise his opinion of that age-old tradition of the rich and famous.

"Noah Samson, you let go of me this instant," Sirena demanded, the evening June breeze instantly clearing her foggy brain.

"Certainly," Noah responded, dropping his arm to his side as the door closed behind them.

She tapped the toe of her shoe against the wraparound front porch, crossed her arms over her chest and glared at him. "What are you doing here?"

He crossed his arms in a parody of hers. "I thought I just made that quite clear. I've come to attempt a reconciliation of our marriage."

"There is no marriage to reconcile!" she exclaimed in an angry whisper, knowing that not only Ben, but her grandmother, mother and aunt were all probably standing at the door with their gossip-twitching ears glued to its solid oak plank. "We've been divorced for two years."

Noah shook his head. "We've been separated for two years. Your Mexican divorce wasn't legal."

"What difference does that make? It's over, Noah. O-V-E-R," she spelled as if he were a dull-witted child. "And it should never have happened in the first place. We are incompatible!"

"We don't know that, Sirena. You hitched up the legs of your designer slacks and ran before we ever had a chance to find out if we were compatible."

"You told me to get out," she reminded yet again, her temper beginning to flare even higher.

"So I made a mistake, and now I'm here to rectify it."

"But I don't *want* it rectified!" she yelled, no longer caring who was listening. "I don't want to be married to you. Now get out, or I'll call the police and have you thrown out."

He shook his head again. "Ophelia says the house is owned jointly by her and your mother, and they have both invited me to stay for as long as I please. You can't throw me out."

"Then I'll leave," she stated, marching purposefully toward the door.

"Fine, but it won't change anything. You still won't be able to get a divorce."

She spun around to face him, her gaze wary. "And why not?"

He raised an index finger and ran it across his bottom lip in a thoughtful gesture. "I did a little checking into the Pennsylvania divorce laws. It seems that I have twenty days to contest your suit for divorce, and my lawyer submitted the appropriate documents this afternoon."

He paused to give her a chance to respond, and when she didn't, he continued. "Since that changes your suit for divorce from no-fault grounds to fault grounds, you must show that we've been separated for three years to get rid of me, and you're short a year. The only way you can waive that time period is to prove that I did something wrong to you, which you can probably do. The twist is, I can also prove that I was wronged, which means we're both at fault. Under the laws of this state, that means neither of us will be granted a divorce. It also means that I can demand that we enroll in marriage counseling, and the judge will order you to attend at least three sessions."

Sirena's eyes narrowed in anger. She wanted to tell him he didn't know what he was talking about, but Jonathan had gone over the laws with her in minute detail, and each and every word Noah had spoken was true. Since she'd never expected him to object—after all, they'd not only been apart for two years, but he'd been about to marry another woman—she'd automatically assumed that she'd be able to coast through a no-fault divorce without complication. She should have known that nothing involving Noah No-middle-initial Samson would ever be uncomplicated.

"What is it you want from me?" she asked plaintively.

"Some time," he answered simply. "I told you at the cabin that I need to finish this chapter of my life and, by damn, I'm going to do it, Sirena, with or without your help."

"I'll go back to Mexico or to the Caribbean to get a divorce," she threatened.

"Fine," Noah responded. "But I would have thought you had more guts than that."

"And just what does that mean?" she demanded shrilly.

"That you don't have what it takes to be a Barrington," he taunted. "I spent the afternoon with your family, and I found out that the Barringtons have always faced their problems head-on. It looks like that noble trait skipped a generation in you, because you keep running away from me instead of staying to fight it out."

Sirena parted her lips to deny his accusation, but she couldn't, because unfortunately it was the truth. She was gutless when it came to Noah. The passion that simmered between them was too strong. His kiss in the dining room had proved that, and if one kiss could render her mindless, what would happen to her if she was forced to be in contact with him day in and day out?

"What about your bride?" she asked. "How's she going to feel about all this?"

"Cynthia and I are over," he replied.

When he'd returned from the cabin he and Cynthia had sat down together and had a long talk. Both had come to the realization that they'd been in love with love and in like with each other. Thankfully, they'd been able to part as friends, and Noah knew that that friendship would be a long and binding one.

His feelings for Sirena, however, were far more complicated. She represented everything he didn't want in a wife. She was spoiled, independent, stubborn and unreasonable. There was also her damn preoccupation with her money, which she seemed to think could buy off any problem that stood in her way. But despite her faults, she made him burn with a grand passion he knew he'd never find with another woman.

Noah had reached the conclusion that he was in lust with Sirena. He also felt that they could build more together if they simply took the time to fight for it. Since he'd known that Sirena would never agree to see him on her own, he'd decided to force the issue by contesting her suit for divorce. Fortunately, the members of her family were willing, if unknowing, accomplices in his quest by opening their home to him.

"So you've come to punish me for making you lose the woman you love," Sirena snapped. "It's a great way to get your revenge, Noah. I screwed up your life, so you're going to screw up mine. I should have know that you'd live by the old proverb of an eye for an eye."

"I'm not seeking revenge," Noah stated calmly. "I'm simply trying to resolve our past. I want us to mend our rifts so we can finally write the end of this chapter and move on with our lives with a clear conscience."

Sirena raked her hand through her hair and walked to the edge of the porch. She wrapped her hands over the railing and gripped it tightly. It would have been much easier for her to swallow his words if she could have convinced herself that he really felt that strongly about repairing their rifts. But how could he make that claim when he hadn't made any effort to come after her two years ago, Mexican divorce or no Mexican divorce? In fact, hadn't she waited in breathless anticipation for just that eventuality?

She pushed the question away, knowing it would only hurt if she explored it. The fact was, she'd divorced Noah and he'd accepted it. Now he was making this absurd demand that they come to grips with their past and resolve their differences. She still thought he was seeking revenge, but it was evident that he was determined. It was also evident that meeting his demand was the only way she was going to get her divorce. Since they'd be chaperoned by the three Barrington matrons, what harm could come from giving him some time?

"Just how much time are we talking about?" she asked in irritated resignation. "I want a specific timetable, Noah."

Noah hadn't realized that he was taut with tension until his body relaxed in response to her question. He was also more than a little suspicious at her easy surrender. "I want a month," he said.

"And at the end of that month, you won't fight my suit for divorce?"

Noah wasn't ready to commit himself that far. "At the end of a month, we'll sit down and determine what's to be done."

It wasn't the answer Sirena wanted, but she decided to accept it. "All right, Noah, I'll give you a month," she said with reluctance, "but only under the condition that you don't try to seduce me into your bed. We know we have no problems in that area that need to be resolved. That part of the chapter is already closed."

Noah nodded his assent, though he had no intention of adhering to her condition. Just looking at Sirena made him ache with desire, and living with her without making love to her would be not only inconceivable but impossible.

"No seduction scenes," he said when her look said his nod hadn't been enough.

"You'll shake on that?"

He extended his hand, while slipping the other behind his back and crossing his fingers. He knew it was a childish gesture, but it was all he could come up with on such short notice.

Sirena accepted his hand and had to fight to keep from jerking her own back when his warm, callused grasp sent shivers of pleasure shooting up her arm. But there would be none of *that*, she insisted. They'd made a bargain, and she'd stick to it if it killed her, which, considering the sudden rise in her hormone level, could be a very real possibility.

When he released her hand she rubbed it against her thigh, saying, "I don't want to build up my family's hopes for a reconciliation, Noah. They need to know that we're simply attempting to make peace with each other, nothing more and nothing less."

"I've already stressed that we're going to *attempt* a reconciliation," Noah countered, not about to give Sirena a semantic loophole. He knew instinctively that if he let her think that divorce was the ultimate outcome she'd never look at their time together objectively. "They're aware that it might not work out. Shall we go in to dinner?" he asked before she could respond, and gestured toward the door gallantly.

"Sure," Sirena answered, but she had a feeling that she'd just stepped onto the path leading to anorexia. Just the thought of food made her feel ill.

If the Barrington women had been pressing their ears against the door, there was no sign of it. The three of them were sitting at the table, chatting pleasantly as they ate.

Tabitha gave Sirena and Noah a smile that said she still thought their kiss had been very romantic. Sirena's grandmother and mother, however, regarded her assessingly. Sirena ignored them by filling her plate with twice as much food as she could possibly eat on a good night, let alone an inauspicious one like this.

Noah resumed his place at the head of the table and dug into his food as if he didn't have a care in the world. Sirena had to admit that his conversation was charming, and even she would have enjoyed it if she could have stopped reminding herself that he was going to be sleeping right next door to her and sharing her bathroom. She wrinkled her nose as she thought of beard stubble in her sink and hair in her shower drain. To her chagrin, neither thought irritated her as much as she would have liked.

She dropped her fork to the table with a clatter when her mother said, "Sirena, I'm very disappointed in you. Why didn't you tell us your divorce wasn't legal?"

"Because it would have spoiled our surprise," Noah inserted smoothly when Sirena's mouth opened and closed in mute response.

Sirena glared at him, despite the fact that he'd just saved her from a fate worse than death—an infamous Barrington lecture, based on an equally infamous belief that a Barrington's life was an open book to every other family member.

"Yes, I didn't want to spoil the surprise," she agreed, giving the three women what she hoped was a sincere smile when she realized they were all staring at her in anticipation of a response. "Noah asked me to keep it a secret until we could announce our..."

"Attempt to reconcile," Noah provided when she choked on the words.

"Oh, it's so romantic," Tabitha murmured dreamily. "Just think, two star-crossed lovers who have found their way back to each other after all this time. Why, it's just like reading a romance novel. How did you find out that your divorce didn't take, Sirena?"

Didn't take? Sirena repeated to herself. *Leave it to Aunt Tabitha....* She gave Noah a vengeful smile as she said, "I'll let you explain, darling."

"Why, darling, I wouldn't even consider taking over center stage," Noah crooned as he leaned toward her and patted her hand in an aggravatingly solicitous gesture.

Noah nearly laughed aloud at Sirena's expression. She was more furious than he'd ever seen her, and if he hadn't been as curious as Tabitha about the answer, he would have dragged her to the nearest bed. Lord, she was beautiful when she was angry.

"Oh, but Noah, I insist," she cooed in a sultry voice that made the hair on the back of his neck stand on end, not to mention a more intimate part of his anatomy. He readjusted the napkin in his lap.

"Sirena, why don't you just tell us?" her grandmother stated impatiently. "After all, Noah is still new to the family and he probably isn't comfortable with us."

Sirena doubted that. In fact, Noah appeared to feel more comfortable here than she did. A chameleon, she thought. That's what he was. A damn chameleon. It was just her luck that she'd gotten involved with a sneaky reptile.

"It all started when I decided to set up a trust fund for the foundation. Jonathan asked for a copy of my divorce decree and . . ."

"And?" her mother encouraged when Sirena's voice trailed off.

"And it might as well have been a taco-filling recipe," Sirena said with a resigned sigh.

Her grandmother gasped.

"That's something I really appreciate," Noah said. "Good food."

"Oh, then you'll love it here, Noah," Sirena's mother said. "We always have good food."

Sirena stabbed her fork into her salad.

The meal progressed at an agonizingly slow pace for Sirena, while Noah appeared to be completely at ease in his role of king for a day. When Mrs. Mullen arrived with a chocolate mousse for dessert, Noah asked her to extend his compliments to the cook. She beamed as she informed him that she was the cook, and Noah took her hand, drawing it to his lips for an Old-World kiss.

The dowdy, heavy-set woman scurried out of the room with a becoming blush that made Sirena mutter to herself in disgust as she glanced around the table and took note of the adoring looks on her family's faces. He'd only been here a few hours and he already had the entire household eating out of the palm of his hand. She decided that this was how General Custer must have felt when he looked up and saw all those Indians coming at him. She set her fork down beside her plate and scooted back her chair, determined to escape this Mad Hatter tea party.

"Sirena, are you all right?" her mother inquired in concern as Sirena's movement drew her attention. "You've barely touched your food."

"I think I must have a touch of the flu," Sirena answered as she rose to her feet. "I'd better call it a night."

"It's all that work," her grandmother scolded fondly. "Child, I don't know why you insist on trying to hold down a man's job. A woman's place is at home, don't you agree, Noah?"

Sirena's gaze was automatically drawn to Noah, who took two bites of his dessert before answering. "Actually, Ophelia, I think a woman's place is where she's the most satisfied. If working provides Sirena with her satisfaction, then that's where she should be."

Sirena could only gape at the man. When they were married she'd literally begged him to let her help at his office, but he'd adamantly refused, telling her that a wife belonged at home, keeping the fires burning and the bed warm. Somehow, she'd always thought that he considered those two chores one and the same.

As if reading her mind, he smiled at her, and then had the audacity to give her a conspiratorial wink. "Go on upstairs, Sirena. I'll check on you before I call it a night."

She wanted to declare him a fraud, but another quick glance around the table told her that any such declaration would be considered the words of a deranged woman.

"Good night," she stated stiffly, chagrined when no one, not even her own mother answered. Noah had already engaged the trio in animated conversation.

In her room, Sirena changed into a sedate flannel nightgown that covered her from neck to ankle, though she knew the night was too warm for it. Noah's threat to check on her had made her don the gown in self-defense, and that made her even more irritated.

She locked both her bedroom door and her door to their shared bathroom and paced the floor, deciding that she'd been absolutely crazy to agree to this reconciliation charade. She should have told Noah to take a flying leap, packed her bags and walked out. In fact, that was exactly what she'd do in the morning.

But even as she made that decision, there was a part of her deep down inside that objected. Noah was claiming that he wanted to resolve their past, and Sirena knew it would be a cleansing act for both of them. So why was she so nervous about it?

Because one of the reasons she'd run two years ago was that she'd started to fall in love with the man. Not an easy, familiar type of love, but a consuming, obsessive one. She'd become jealous of everything in Noah's life, from his business to their landlady, who'd been far too young and flirtatious for Sirena's peace of mind. For the first time in her life she'd realized there was something her money couldn't buy, namely Noah's love. It was a fact that had brought her to earth with a jolt.

She was still pacing when she heard Noah enter the bath, and she quickly scrambled into bed and pulled the pillow over her head so she wouldn't overhear his nightly ritual. The next thing she knew it was morning.

WITH A SIGH OF RELIEF, Sirena got up and got ready for work. But if the night before had been a shocker, the scene that awaited her downstairs beat it hands down.

Jonathan was pacing the hallway at the foot of the stairs, and Sirena could only stare at him in stunned disbelief. Immaculate, never-a-hair-out-of-place Jonathan

Harcourt, Esq. looked as if he'd been picked up by his heels and shaken.

His blond hair stood on end, and she realized it was because his hand was raking through it nonstop. He hadn't shaved, and his shirttail was half in and half out of the waistband of a rumpled pair of slacks.

"My word, Jonathan, what's wrong?" Sirena asked in concern as she hurried down the stairs toward him.

"Dammit, Sirena, I've been trying to reach you since last night. First Ben told me you were dining. Then he told me you'd retired early. Even when I told him it was an emergency, he refused to disturb you." Jonathan took her arm and propelled her into the sitting room. "That man takes too much upon himself. You'd better do something about him."

Sirena sat down on the small love seat Jonathan led her to and glanced at her hands, unable to control the twitch of her lips at his aggrieved tone when he referred to the butler. He and Ben had been waging a civilized war of words ever since she and Jonathan had started dating. She knew it was Ben's way of communicating his disapproval of her relationship with Jonathan, whom he constantly referred to as the old coot.

Though Sirena supposed she should be angry with Ben, she couldn't find the heart to take him to task. Ever since she started dating, he'd appointed himself her guardian angel, and there had always been a certain comfort in knowing that whenever she went out Ben would be waiting up for her when she came home. He'd also rescued her from a few far too ardent suitors over the years. Too bad he hadn't gone with her to Bedford so he could have rescued her from Noah.

"Ben didn't mean to be rude, Jonathan. He's just overprotective of me. Now, tell me what's wrong."

"Your ex-husband is what's wrong!" Jonathan exclaimed. "He's fighting your divorce action."

"I know," Sirena stated.

"You know? How?"

"He's here."

"Here? In this house?" Jonathan asked, as if trying to disprove her revelation.

Sirena nodded. "He arrived yesterday."

"Well, you have to throw him out. If you don't, we'll never convince a judge to give you a divorce."

"I can't throw him out," Sirena said with a resigned sigh. "Mother and Grandmother have invited him to stay, and they do own the house."

"Then you must leave immediately."

"I can't do that, either." When he frowned in confusion, she said, "I told Noah I'd give him a month to resolve our differences."

Jonathan stared at her as if she'd just announced that she'd committed some heinous crime. "You aren't serious."

"I'm perfectly serious," Sirena stated. "Noah is prepared to fight me tooth and nail unless I agree to his demand. The way I see it, I give him a few weeks to put the past to rest. Then he'll be amicable about the divorce."

"And if he's not?" Jonathan countered as he sat down beside her and caught her hands in his. "What if he decides that he wants to remain married?"

Sirena chuckled ruefully. "Don't be silly. Noah and I can't be in the same room for five minutes without fighting. When I walked out on him, I wounded his ego. He just wants it soothed."

"It's more likely that he wants his pocketbook soothed," Jonathan grumbled. "Sirena, what you're doing is dangerous. If you reside under the same roof with him, you're acknowledging that he's your husband. You're giving him ammunition to take you to court and stake a claim on your money."

"Noah has no designs on my money," Sirena immediately objected. When Jonathan looked doubtful, she said, "I know it's true, Jonathan. I know the man."

"You lived with him for three weeks. You couldn't possibly know him, and even if you are right, what about me?" Jonathan demanded. "Do you really expect me to sit by and let him live here without complaint? You know how I feel about you. I want to marry you."

"That might be a bit difficult, considering the fact that she's already married to me," a deep voice drawled.

The bones in Sirena's neck made a cracking sound as she snapped her head toward the doorway. Noah—dressed in denims so tight they looked painted on, and a T-shirt that was even more body hugging—was lounging against the doorjamb with a nonchalance that belied the hard gleam in his blue eyes. Sirena gulped. He not only looked deadly, but gorgeous enough to swoon over.

He levered himself upright and strolled into the room, his thumbs hooked in the front pockets of his jeans. "Ben said we had company, Sirena, so I came to pay my respects."

Sirena grimaced inwardly as Jonathan sputtered, "This is your husband?"

Noah arched a brow, and his voice dropped into that deceptively soft tone that she'd last heard at the chapel. "Yes, I'm her husband. And you're . . ."

"My attorney and my friend," Sirena supplied warily as she watched Noah's approach, sensing menace in his loose-limbed walk.

"Dammit, Sirena, I'm more than that and you know it," Jonathan railed.

Sirena's head snapped back toward Jonathan in shock. He'd actually yelled at her!

"Well, more than friend and attorney, you are talking to my wife, and I would suggest that you do so politely," Noah stated as he arrived at the love seat and placed a possessive hand on Sirena's shoulder.

Sirena glanced up at him. She could see the male challenge in his eyes, and knew instinctively that he was more dangerous at this moment than she'd ever seen him.

She quickly switched her attention to Jonathan, and her mouth dropped open as she watched him rise to his feet, his hands clenched at his sides in readiness for battle. She expected caveman tactics from Noah. After all, they were a despot's stock-in-trade. But Jonathan had always been a gentleman! He was also no physical match for Noah.

Noah's grip on her shoulder tightened when Jonathan said, "I don't take orders from you, and you are interrupting a private meeting. I'd suggest you leave. In fact, I'd suggest that you go upstairs, pack your bags and get the hell out of here."

"And if I don't want to get the hell out of here?" Noah drawled.

"Then I may have to help you on your way," Jonathan drawled back.

Dumbfounded, Sirena glanced back and forth between them. She couldn't believe they were acting like two grade-school bullies fighting over control of the playground. She also knew she had to do something before there was bloodshed, but since she'd never been the object of a dispute between two men, she had no idea how to handle them.

To her relief Ben came to the rescue by stepping into the room and calmly asking, "Should I have coffee served, Miss Sirena?"

"No," Sirena stated firmly as she rose to her feet and sent a scathing glare at Noah, then at Jonathan. "I'll be leaving for work in just a moment, Ben, and I'm sure these two *gentlemen* will be doing the same. In fact, why don't you see Mr. Harcourt to the door."

"But, Sirena, we need to talk," Jonathan objected.

"Yes, Jonathan, we do," she agreed. "However, this is neither the time nor the place. I'll call you at the office."

Jonathan opened his mouth as if to disagree, but seemed to think better of it as he eyed her stony expression. "Fine. I'll expect your call."

She gave a curt nod, and after he'd exited, she turned on Noah. His smug grin made her want to kick him in the shin, and she was sorely tempted to pick up the nearby Ming vase and crack it over his head.

"Just what did you think you were proving with that little scene?" she asked in exasperation.

"I was defending your honor."

"Defending my honor?" she repeated in disbelief. "You are crazy, Noah. In fact, you've gone beyond crazy. They haven't even come up with a medical term for your mental aberration!"

"*My* mental aberration?" he mocked. "Good, Lord, Sirena, that man is old enough to be your father. Watching him put the moves on you was positively sickening. Not only that, he yelled at you."

Sirena drew in a deep breath and counted to ten, but it didn't help. In fact, the action only made her more angry.

"First off," she stated tightly as she held up an index finger, "Jonathan is not old enough to be my father. Secondly," she continued, holding up her middle finger, "he was not putting the moves on me. He was merely expressing his feelings for me, which happen to be very deep." Her ring finger went up with, "Thirdly, why shouldn't he yell at me? You do it all the time."

She wanted to scream when he said, "Of course, I yell at you. You're my wife."

"I am not your wife!"

He grinned. "If you're not, then why are you yelling at me?"

"Because you are the most infuriating, exasperating, annoying man I have ever known."

His grin widened. "I knew if you gave yourself half a chance you'd begin to like me."

Sirena tossed her arm into the air in defeat. "I give up. There's no talking to you. You are going to do what you want to do, regardless of my feelings. You just don't care."

"Oh, I care," Noah said. "If I didn't I wouldn't have interrupted you and the old coot."

"Ben!" Sirena exclaimed as she heard the familiar description. "He put you up to this. Jonathan's right. I need to do something about him."

"Don't be ridiculous, Sirena. Loyal butlers are hard to come by these days. Just ask Ophelia. She told me all about it. She also agrees that the old coot is an old coot, and no match for a passionate woman like you. You need someone young and—"

"Just stop right there, Noah Samson," Sirena ordered, her temper having escalated to the point of no return. "It's bad enough that you've come barging into my life and turned it upside down, but when you start discussing my love life with my grandmother, you are making yourself a target for cold-blooded murder."

His grin faded and he frowned at her in concern. "You're really upset."

"Gosh, how did you ever come to that conclusion?" Sirena said in disgust.

"I'm sorry, Sirena. I didn't mean to upset you. When Ben and your grandmother said you'd been dating this guy, I thought I should help you explain having your husband in the house. I only meant to help you out of an awkward situation."

"By making it more awkward?" she asked as she raked her hand through her hair. She wanted to stay angry with him, but he looked so darn contrite that her temper began to flag despite her efforts to keep it fueled. She gave a weary shake of her head. "Since it's apparent that you had a great deal of encouragement from the Barrington peanut gallery, I'll forgive you this time, but don't let it happen again, Noah. I am quite capable of not only handling my own awkward situations, but defending my honor. Now, if you'll excuse me, I have to get to work."

She'd just reached the doorway when he said, "Sirena?"

"What?" she asked as she stopped and glanced over her shoulder at him in resignation, wondering what bombshell he intended to drop this time.

"Thanks for telling Harcourt I wasn't interested in your money. That means a lot to me."

Any remaining ire faded as Sirena gazed at him. He'd stuffed his hands into his pants pockets, which was quite a feat considering the jeans' intimate fit, and his lips were curved into an almost shy smile. It was the first time Sirena had ever seen him look vulnerable, and it caused an intense feeling of protectiveness to surge through her.

Confused and more than a little frightened by the sensation, she responded with, "We both know that that's another area that doesn't need to be resolved between us. Have a good day, Noah."

"You, too," he murmured, but she was already gone.

He walked to the window and waited until Sirena climbed into an ancient Toyota that had definitely seen better days and drove away. The poor little rich girl was proving to be full of surprises, and Noah was becoming more and more intrigued.

When her car disappeared from sight, he stuffed his hands back into his pockets and strolled out of the room, whistling a cheerful tune. Now that he'd seen the old coot, he knew he didn't have any competition. But just to be on the safe side, he decided it was time to do a little old-fashioned courting of his wife. He'd take a few days to clear up everything at the office and then he'd pull out all the stops.

5

SIRENA HAD NEVER HAD a migraine headache, but she was sure that the throbbing in her head had to be one. Her day had gone from bad to worse. When she called Jonathan, he'd insisted on coming to her office to "straighten things out," which had resulted in a major confrontation.

She still couldn't believe that nice, calm, steady Jonathan had turned out to be as unreasonable as Noah. When he'd given her the ultimatum of "That man or me," Sirena had been amazed at how easy it had been to make a choice. She also knew she deserved Jonathan's accusation of leading him on. Even if she hadn't made any verbal commitment to him, she'd known how he felt about her and she'd complacently straddled the fence. By the time he left, she'd been more upset with herself than with him.

On the heels of his departure had come a call from a city inspector regarding the old hotel she'd purchased and was trying to get licensed for a long-term shelter for the homeless. He'd given her a list of improvements on the building that would have to be accomplished before he'd even consider recommending licensure, and Sirena had had to bite her tongue to keep from railing at the man. It was the third such list in as many months from as many different inspectors. Every time she met one inspector's demands, along came another with more. She knew she was getting the runaround, but she hadn't figured out how to stop it without endangering the project.

Leaning back wearily in her chair, she heard a knock on her door and called, "Come in." Her administrative assistant, Margie Swenson, entered with the largest Boston fern Sirena had ever seen. "What in the world is that?" Sirena asked.

"A Boston fern," Margie answered with a grin as she carefully placed the plant on Sirena's desk. "There's a card."

Sirena leaned forward and retrieved the card. She shook her head when she opened it and saw the bold handwriting. The message read: "Sometimes words aren't enough. I'm sorry about this morning. Noah."

"Well, who's it from?" Margie asked impatiently.

Sirena glanced up at her, absently saying, "Noah."

"Who's Noah?" Margie asked.

"My husband."

"Husband!" Margie yelped, her brown eyes as wide as saucers. "When did you get married?"

"Two years ago," Sirena answered. "I thought I was divorced, but I just found out that I'm not."

Margie tossed her long brown hair over her shoulder and sat down in the chair in front of Sirena's desk. "This sounds like a story I want to hear. Tell me all about it."

"There isn't much to tell," Sirena said. "I went to Mexico to get a divorce, but when Jonathan started to set up the trust fund for the foundation he discovered the divorce wasn't legal."

Sirena frowned at Margie when the young woman commented, "That must have shaken up the old coot."

"I'm going to murder Ben," Sirena muttered irritably.

"Don't be melodramatic," Margie said with a chuckle. "Besides, loyal butlers are hard—"

"—to come by these days," Sirena finished, her frown deepening. "When did you start talking to my grandmother?"

"Since the day we opened the doors," Margie answered as she crossed her legs and began to swing her foot. "She checks in three or four times a week to make sure you're okay. It must be nice to have such a sweet grandmother."

Sirena only nodded, because she knew her grandmother's motives weren't that uncomplicated. "Who else in the family are you routinely in contact with?"

Margie shrugged. "Your mother and Tabitha, of course. Your brother Stefan gives me a call about once a month, and your brother Damon calls every two or three months."

Sirena didn't know whether she should be furious or whether she should just sit down and cry. She knew her family loved her, but they refused to believe that she was all grown up and capable of taking care of herself. It was the reason she hadn't let any of them invest one cent in the foundation, not even through donations. It would have been inviting interference.

As if suddenly realizing the import of her confession, Margie said, "Sirena, I never discuss the foundation's business with them. I only assure them that you're okay. They worry about you."

"Yeah," Sirena said, but her laugh was brittle.

Fortunately, she wasn't required to say more, because the receptionist buzzed to announce that Margie had a call, and she hurried back to her desk to take it. Sirena sighed as she reached out and stroked one of the long fronds on the fern Noah had sent her.

She knew the plant represented more than an apology. It was also Noah's way of saying he remembered that she didn't care for cut flowers. She couldn't help but recall the circumstances under which she'd told him that fact.

He'd taken her to the grocery store. Since grocery shopping in the Barrington household had always been the cook's duty, it had been an adventure for her. Noah had indulgently followed her though the store without complaint as she prowled the aisles with as much enthusiasm as a kid turned loose in a candy store.

When they finally reached the checkout stand their basket had been overflowing. A refrigerator of cut flowers had been nearby, and Noah had teasingly asked, "Don't you think we need a bouquet or two for the crowning touch to this mountain?"

"No," Sirena had answered as she'd eyed the colorful display. "I don't like cut flowers. It makes me sad to watch them die. I like living plants that you can water and nurture."

The next day he'd come home with a bright yellow mum in a pot. Tears welled up in Sirena's eyes as she remembered how hard it had been to leave that plant behind.

"Damn you, Noah Samson," she whispered as she dashed at an errant tear that began to roll down her cheek. "You're more dangerous than I thought you were, but I'm not going to let you get to me."

However, he was already getting to her, and she knew she had to keep her distance. If she didn't she'd only be setting herself up for a fall, because, she reminded herself, Noah was out for revenge.

IT WAS NEARLY NOON when Noah parked at the curb and studied the old tumbledown building that sat on the perimeter of downtown Harrisburg. He hadn't expected Barrington Foundation to look like this. He'd figured that Sirena would have built herself a Taj Mahal to play in.

He drummed his fingers against the steering wheel as he realized that from the moment he'd first learned about

Sirena's background he'd tucked her into a neat little niche and concentrated on that one dimension instead of the woman as a whole. It was becoming more and more apparent that he'd underestimated her, but he wouldn't be making that mistake any longer.

For the past two days he and Sirena had been playing cat and mouse with each other. He'd purposely risen early each day and started on the eighty-mile drive to his office in Hagerstown before she awakened. She seemed to be purposely coming home late each night so that dinner was already in progress when she arrived, and she'd excuse herself and disappear upstairs before dessert was served.

Noah knew that the female Barringtons had been watching them curiously, their heads bobbing from Sirena to him and back to Sirena as if they were viewing a tennis match. But he'd decided that when he brought the game to an end, he had to be in a position to devote the majority of his time to Sirena. Only this morning had he finished setting up his office so that it could be run by telephone.

He glanced down at his watch, noted the hour and climbed out of his car, determined to take his wife to lunch. But when he walked into the reception area, all he could do was stare in openmouthed astonishment. The large room was overflowing with people, many of whom had questionable grooming habits, and he was greeted at the reception desk by a full-grown tiger.

He took a giant step backward from the animal, wondering if he was hallucinating; no one else in the room seemed aware of the big cat. He glanced down quickly when he felt a tug on his suit coat.

A small grimy boy of about five announced, "I have to potty."

One look at the tiger, who chose that moment to run a long tongue across his bottom lip in a ravenous gesture, made Noah decide that the boy should be his first priority.

"Okay, kid," he said as he took the urchin's hand. "Do you know where the men's room is?"

"Down the hall and to the right," a woman in the crowd offered in a bored tone.

Noah took the boy down the hall, found the rest room and waited. When the child was done, Noah lifted him to the sink so he could wash his hands, resisting the urge to stick the rest of him under the faucet and give him a good scrub.

"Where's your mother?" he asked as they walked back to Sirena's office.

"Don't know," the child replied.

"Didn't she come with you?"

"No."

Noah frowned as he opened the door and the boy rushed to a corner that was filled with toys and children's books. He once again approached the reception desk, which was, to his relief, now staffed by a harried-looking woman instead of a man-eating tiger. He must have been hallucinating.

He cleared his throat when she didn't look up.

"Oh, I'm sorry!" she exclaimed when her inquisitive brown eyes flowed down him, taking in his three-piece suit. "May I help you?"

"I'm looking for Sirena Barrington."

"I'm afraid that she's not available at the moment. She's supervising the inoculations. I'm Margie Swenson, her administrative assistant. Perhaps I can help."

"No. I'm . . . a friend of hers," he said, not sure that Sirena had informed her staff that she had a husband, and not about to embarrass her if she hadn't. "What kind of inoculations is she supervising?"

The young woman reached up to toss her long brown hair over her shoulder as she rattled off, "Measles, mumps, polio, chicken pox, tetanus. You name it, we're giving it."

Noah glanced around him. "I thought she might be free to join me for lunch, but from the looks of this crowd that's probably out of the question."

The woman nodded her agreement. "There's no time for lunch on inoculation day. If you'd like to give me your name, though, I'll let her know you're here."

"No, that's all right, Ms Swenson," Noah said, lifting from the pile on the woman's desk a brochure that supposedly outlined Barrington Foundation's services. "I'll just hang around until she's available."

"That could be the rest of the day," she warned.

"That's all right. I don't have anything better to do."

He found an empty chair and opened the brochure. A quick glance through the material made him arch his brows in surprise. It appeared that the foundation not only provided free inoculations once a month, but everything from job training and employment services to child care to mental health counseling to shelters for the homeless, and that was just on the human side. It was also actively involved in animal protection and environmental matters. Noah had to admit that he was truly impressed.

He was still concentrating on the brochure when he felt another tug on his jacket, and he smiled when he recognized his young compatriot. "Need to go to the bathroom again?"

The boy shook his head as he scrambled onto Noah's lap and opened the book in his hand. He pointed to the first word in the sentence. "What's that word?"

"It," Noah answered. "Can you read?"

"No, but my grandma says I'll learn when I go to school. That's only two months away."

"That sounds exciting."

"Uh-huh. What's that word?" the boy asked, pointing to the second word in the sentence.

Noah unconsciously tousled the child's hair as he said, "Was. Would you like me to read you the story?"

"Yeah."

Noah felt a strange satisfaction when the boy settled back against his chest. He began to read aloud, unaware of the rest of the children who crept closer and settled into a semicircle around his feet.

And that was how Sirena found him two and a half hours and twelve books later, his one urchin having been replaced several times over. The children clustered around him were gazing up at him in rapt attention, and Sirena's heart gave a strange little lurch at the picture he presented.

"How long has Noah been here," she asked Margie, who was sitting with her chin propped in her hands and watching Noah with the look of a devoted follower.

"That's Noah?" Margie gasped as she glanced up at Sirena in surprise. "He didn't tell me he was your husband. He just said he was a friend."

Sirena patted the tiger's head as he appeared from out of nowhere and rubbed against her legs. "That's Noah. How long has he been here?"

"Since lunch. I offered to tell you he was here, but he said he'd wait. It's all right, isn't it?"

"Yeah, it's all right," Sirena murmured, her gaze straying over each and every one of the children before finally returning to Noah and the little girl tucked securely in one crook of his arm.

He'd shed his suit coat, unbuttoned his vest and rolled up his shirtsleeves. The raggedly dressed little girl looked perfectly at home nestled against him, and that brought unexpected tears to Sirena's eyes. She'd never envisioned Noah with children, and now that she saw him with them, she suddenly realized that she'd always concentrated on the bitterness in their marriage and had ignored the tenderness and gentleness.

"If he asks for me again, let me know," she told Margie, reluctant to interrupt his impromptu story hour.

"I sure will, but I have a feeling he's not going to move a muscle until there isn't a kid in the room."

Margie's prediction came true. It was nearly six in the evening when she pried the last little tyke out of Noah's arms, and he glanced at his watch before giving her a sheepish grin.

"Time flies when you're having fun."

Margie chuckled as the little girl wound her legs around her waist and her arms around her neck. "It sure does, and your wife looks like she's about ready to drop. If I hustle her out here, do you think you can manage to drag her home and put some food in her mouth?"

"I'll give it my best shot," he said, pleased that the woman was aware of his and Sirena's relationship.

Margie disappeared and the tiger wandered into the room. Noah would have sworn the big cat was purring as he strolled right up to him and sat back on his haunches, his tongue once again slipping out in that hungry gesture while his tail twitched from side to side. Noah remained completely still, wondering if tigers purred before they attacked their victims. If so, he figured he was dead meat.

"His name's Rufus," Sirena announced, and Noah glanced toward her in surprise. She was slipping out of a white laboratory coat, revealing a simple white blouse and navy blue skirt. "He's toothless, clawless, nearly blind and half crippled with arthritis. We rescued him from his former owner, who abused him. I tried to get him into a zoo, but no one wanted a geriatric, sexually altered Siberian tiger that can't breed, so I got a permit to keep him. He normally lives at the mansion, but we had some diseased trees that needed to be sprayed and the vet said the pesticide might harm him. He's been living here with my administrative assistant until we feel it's safe to take him back home."

"Your administrative assistant lives in the building?" Noah questioned, while tentatively reaching out to pet the tiger. The animal rubbed his chin against Noah's knee and licked his hand with a tongue rougher than any sandpaper he'd ever encountered.

Sirena nodded. "We have an overnight shelter for the homeless in the basement. Margie oversees it in exchange for free room and board."

"So the poor little rich girl has finally found a few causes to keep herself occupied." Noah regretted the words the instant they were out of his mouth. "I'm sorry, Sirena. That was uncalled for."

She shrugged nonchalantly, but refused to look at him, knowing that her hurt would be shining in her eyes. She pretended to sort through the mail on the receptionist's desk. "That's all right, Noah. I suppose the only scale you have to measure me against is the person you knew two years ago."

"It was still uncalled for," he said, rising to his feet and walking toward her. He caught her chin in his hand and tilted her head upward so he could see her face. "I wouldn't want to be measured against the man I was two years ago, because when I look back on him, I find I don't like him very much. How about if we call a truce and promise ourselves that we'll look at each other for what we are today, and to hell with the past."

"Okay," she agreed, feeling breathless as she gazed into his handsome face. When he lowered his head slightly, she thought he might kiss her. She found herself yearning for it to happen, in spite of the fact that she'd insisted their relationship remain strictly platonic.

But he didn't kiss her. Instead he asked, "How long has it been since you've gone out for pizza?"

"Pizza?" she echoed, unable to even call an image of the food to mind beneath his mesmerizing indigo gaze. She'd forgotten how beautifully expressive his eyes were, and her fingers itched to stroke the long, thick black lashes that framed them.

He grinned at her. "Pizza, Sirena. It's round, covered with tomato sauce and a million other totally fattening but delicious morsels."

"I haven't had pizza since . . ."

"Since you lived with me?" he guessed when she didn't complete the sentence. She nodded and he chuckled, recalling that he'd been the one to introduce her to the delicacy. He'd been shocked to discover that she'd never eaten it and had decided that being born with a silver spoon in your mouth wasn't all that appetizing. "Then I think it's way past the time that you indulged yourself."

"Are you brave enough to call home and tell the Barrington matrons that we've decided to eat out?"

He frowned in consternation. "They expect you to check in?"

"They expect *us* to check in, Noah."

"But we're adults!"

"We also live under their roof, and Mrs. Mullen cooks for all of us unless she's told otherwise."

He jammed a hand deep into his pants pocket and jingled his change. "If that was supposed to make me feel guilty, it worked."

Sirena chuckled and reached up to pat his cheek. "Welcome to the Barrington guilt club. Believe me, I'm a charter member."

He caught her hand and entwined his fingers with hers as he searched her face, deciding that Margie Swenson had been right. She did look as if she were ready to drop, but he suspected that it wasn't just a hard day at the office that had put the soft bruises beneath her eyes and given life to the lines of fatigue that bracketed her mouth. Along with a surge of concerned tenderness came the knowledge that he was partially responsible for her weariness.

Though he was developing a great fondness for the elder Barrington women, he was well aware of the vein of steel that existed within each of them, even sweet, eccentric Tabitha. He also knew that Sirena was quite capable of holding her own with them, because she'd always been able to stand toe to toe with him. However, even he would have had difficulty in dealing with the three matrons, as Sirena had so aptly called them, if they decided to gang up on him. And that was exactly what they'd been doing to Sirena, at least on a subliminal level. He'd also been encouraging their torment.

What she needed was a night out, he decided. An evening where she could just sit back, relax and not have to be on guard against every spoken word.

He absently stroked his thumb across her smooth knuckles as he asked, "Do you think I'll be tarred and feathered and thrown out of the house if I'm rude enough to call home and announce that I'm taking my wife out to dinner?"

Sirena shook her head. *His wife.* Why did those two words sound so good? Feel so good? They shouldn't but they did, and though Sirena knew it was wrong, she allowed herself a moment to revel in the sensation.

"I think you, of all people, could get away with it," she told him. "You've charmed the socks off the three of them."

He reached out to tuck a lock of hair behind her ear. "I suppose that's a compliment. Unfortunately, those aren't the socks I want to charm off."

Sirena once again became busy with the mail, and Noah knew he'd crossed over the invisible line she'd drawn between them. He sighed as he stuck his hands into his pockets.

"Sirena, don't pull away from me like that," he pleaded quietly when she continued to ignore him. "I hate you withdrawing from me as much now as I did two years ago."

She glanced up at him, her eyes widened in disbelief. "I never withdrew from you."

"The hell you didn't. I'd ask you a question, and you'd crawl into that shell. The only way I could get you out of it was to fight with you or drag you off to bed."

She frowned and shook her head in abject confusion. "I wasn't withdrawing. I was thinking. You were asking me questions that I didn't have answers to. For the first time I was being forced to evaluate my life, and I realized that you were right when you accused me of being shallow. I had no direction. No purpose. If it hadn't been for you, Barrington Foundation might never have been born, and I must thank you for making me see that I was obligated to do more with my money than sit around and let my accountants count it."

It was Noah's turn to peer at her in disbelief, but he didn't know how to respond, because he suddenly understood that he hadn't accused her of being shallow for any other reason than it was guaranteed to infuriate her.

Feeling more awkward than he had in years, Noah muttered, "Well, you're welcome. I'd better make that call."

Sirena, feeling awkward herself, went to say good-night to her staff, while wondering if pleading a headache would get her out of her dinner date with Noah. When she returned, Noah had buttoned his vest, rolled down his shirtsleeves and slipped into his suit coat. He looked so handsome that he took her breath away.

"I feel like David facing Goliath," she muttered to herself as she donned her own jacket and slung her purse over her shoulder. When she walked across the room to join him, she made a mental note to buy a sling shot first thing in the morning.

NOAH, STILL CONCERNED about Sirena's apparent weariness, had decided that she didn't need a night out at a noisy family pizzeria. After he'd made his call to the Barrington mansion, Margie had wandered into the room and told him about a nearby restaurant that served both pizza and traditional Italian meals and was not a family hangout.

When he told Sirena that they'd take his car and he'd drive her to work the next morning, she didn't even bat an eye, which made him more convinced than ever that a quiet restaurant was in order. If he'd learned nothing else during their three-week marriage, it was that Sirena didn't like to be dependent upon anyone, not even for a ride, which had resulted in one of their many battles.

She'd left her car in Bedford when she went with him to Maryland. She'd begged, cajoled and eventually screamed when he refused to take her back to get it. Though he'd told her he was just too busy building his business to make the trip, the truth was he'd been terrified that once she had wheels of her own, she'd drive right out of his life. He found it ironic that in the long run—or rather the short run—she'd still managed to run away. Would she have stayed if he'd given in and let her be mobile?

He cast a furtive glance toward her, only to find her sitting bolt upright in her seat and staring straight ahead. He wanted to reach out and stroke her, make her relax. Instead, he returned his attention to the road.

Sirena was struggling with her own inner turmoil as she kept her eyes glued to the pavement. When Noah was around her, she was as aware of him as of an irritating toothache, and not even aspirin was going to soothe the pain. Her entire body ached with a need that she absolutely refused to acknowledge, no matter how much it clamored for her to do so.

While she kept telling herself she was crazy for accepting his dinner invitation, she also knew that at some point she was going to have to spend time with him. If she didn't he wouldn't leave at the end of the agreed month, and she knew she didn't have the physical or the emotional stamina to handle his hanging around indefinitely.

When Noah pulled into the parking lot of a small Italian restaurant, she leaped out of the car and hurried toward the entrance, determined to get inside before he had the opportunity to touch her.

But he caught up with her at the door, grasped her elbow in one hand and the door handle in the other, bringing her to a stop as he said in exasperation, "Sirena, I know you're a liberated woman, but are you going to grow a wart on the end of your nose if you let me play the role of a chivalrous escort?"

She raised her head, a snappish retort on the tip of her tongue, but it died when she met his eyes. Neon lights did wonderful things to them. They sparkled and danced and teased at her senses. She lowered her gaze to his sensuous lips, and her stomach started a downward plunge, reminding her of the descending ball in Times Square on New Year's Eve. She even had the fireworks to go along with it.

"What is it, mermaid?" he asked coaxingly. "What has you as skittish as a long-tailed cat in a roomful of rocking chairs?"

"That's a terribly trite saying," she murmured as she returned her gaze to his.

He gave a negligent shrug as he searched her face. "It may be trite, but it's true. You dashed across the parking lot as if you were in training for the Olympics. I know you have to be hungry after the long day you've put in, but whatever happened to decorum?"

"Decorum?" she repeated inanely. "I never had any decorum around you."

His satyr's grin arrowed its way right down to the tips of her toes, and she shivered when he leaned toward her to whisper throatily, "Honey, you always had plenty of decorum. It was just a little more bourgeois at sometimes than others."

Sirena knew she was blushing to the roots of her hair at his teasing innuendo, but she really didn't care. His words had made her feel womanly and sexy, and she hadn't truly felt that way since she left him. "Is sex all you ever think about?"

"No," he answered as he opened the door and led her inside. "You just bring out the best in me."

Sirena couldn't help it. She giggled at his comment and felt herself relaxing when he chuckled and draped his arm around her shoulders, giving her a fond squeeze.

As the waitress led them to a small, intimate booth overlooking the wide Susquehanna River, Sirena was reminded of their first meal together in Bedford. It, too, had been Italian, and she found herself yearning to share plates of spaghetti, she slurping off his fork and he slurping off hers, as they'd done that night.

It seemed that Noah was on the same wavelength, because he said, "This will be our second real dinner out together, and I already feel as if we're in a rut. I guess I should have opted for Chinese."

"This is fine," she said as she lifted the menu and scanned it, though every word was blurred by those haunting memories from the past. "You wanted pizza, right?"

"I wanted to have dinner with you. Order whatever you like."

Whatever she liked was a stroll down memory lane. It would be so easy to order spaghetti and then let the evening conclude as it had in the past—having Noah for dessert in a deliciously rumpled bed. It would be easy, but also deadly. She released an inward sigh of resignation.

"I'd like a pizza with everything on it," she announced. "As you've probably realized, pizza isn't in Mrs. Mullen's repertoire of gourmet meals. By the way, how did the matrons deal with our impromptu night out?"

"Tabitha answered the phone," he replied, feeling disappointed that she hadn't decided on spaghetti. "I bet you can't guess what she said."

"Oh, how romantic!" Sirena exclaimed in a perfect mimicry of her aunt.

Noah laughed. "I didn't know you were psychic."

She arched one delicately winged brow, and Noah clenched his hands into fists to keep from reaching out and stroking it.

"You don't have to be psychic to second-guess Aunt Tabitha," she said wryly, before quickly amending with, "unless it comes to poker, of course. You do know that she's an amazing poker player, don't you?"

"Tabitha?" Noah questioned disbelievingly.

"Tabitha," Sirena affirmed. "In fact, she nearly won the national title in the amateur playoffs last year."

"That sweet little thing is a card shark?"

"That sweet little thing would take you to the cleaners without batting an eye. She's ruthless."

"I'll be damned," Noah said. Then he asked, "She's Ophelia's daughter and your father's sister, right?"

"Uh-huh," Sirena answered after taking a sip of her water.

"Why hasn't she ever married?"

"She was engaged once, but her fiancé was killed in an automobile accident. She never found anyone to replace him."

"A victim of tragedy," Noah murmured thoughtfully. "Somehow, she fits the role and it explains a lot."

"A lot of what?" Sirena asked, curious.

"Her preoccupation with our nonexistent sex life." He smiled devilishly when Sirena frowned at him. "Tabitha has breakfast with me every morning, and she's very upset with you. She's horrified that you're not sharing your husband's bed, and even more horrified that you aren't supervising his most essential meal of the day."

"And you assured her that you were a grown man and quite capable of supervising your own breakfast, right?" she inquired dryly, deciding that the better part of valor would be to ignore the first part of his declaration.

His eyes glinted laughter. "Of course not. I rather like being the center of attention."

Sirena gave a disapproving shake of her head. "You're incorrigible, Noah, and you should be ashamed of yourself for egging on Aunt Tabitha."

"Mmm, maybe, but I think Tabitha enjoys being all aflutter. It livens up her life."

Sirena knew she should scold him, but she suspected he was right. Her aunt had been at loose ends since Sirena's brothers left home, and she'd always been overly devoted to the male members of the family. Noah would be a good distraction for her.

"Aunt Tabitha has quite a head for business," Sirena told him as she took a sip of the hearty red wine he poured into her glass. "I've tried to get her to supervise some of the fund-raising drives for the foundation, but she knows that Grandmother disapproves of what I'm doing, so she's reluctant to get involved."

"Ophelia's against the foundation?" Noah questioned in surprise.

"Not the foundation, but my active role in it," Sirena stated. "Barrington women are supposed to get married, have babies and be devoted wives, while their men go out and face the big, bad world. She makes my life as miserable as she can at any given opportunity."

"So why do you continue to live there?"

Sirena smiled ruefully. "Guilt. Every time I pack to leave, they tell me how they'll worry about me if I'm all alone, and for Grandmother, it's a very real fear. Her daughter, Delia, was kidnapped when she was three. Evidently the kidnappers didn't know that she had a congenital heart condition that required daily medication. She died, and they never caught the people responsible."

"Oh, my God," Noah whispered in horror.

Sirena nodded her agreement before saying, "It happened forty years ago, but Grandmother still has nightmares about it. Sometimes I'll wake up in the middle of the night and find her sitting by the side of my bed. She always says that she just wants to know that I'm safe. I hate that."

Noah saw the tears in Sirena's eyes and he reached across the table to catch her hand. Squeezing it, he said, "My poor little rich girl."

Sirena's gaze rose to his face and she smiled, because for once the words hadn't been demeaning but spoken in true sympathy. She turned her hand and linked her fingers with his.

"You once told me that being filthy rich isn't all it's cracked up to be," she said, unable to control the catch in her voice.

"I'm finding out just how right I was," Noah said, wishing that they weren't sitting in a restaurant, but somewhere private where he could pull her into his arms and comfort her. "Are you afraid, Sirena?"

Sirena told herself the question was generic, but as she searched his face she couldn't deny the concern she saw in his eyes any more than she could deny the crazy feelings that the emotion stirred up inside of her, especially when there was a part of her that was afraid and always would be. Delia's story had been drummed into her from the time she'd been able to have even a passing understanding of danger. On a rational level she knew that her fear was unreasonable, but it was still there.

"Not when I'm with you," she confessed so softly that the words were no more than a breath of air.

But Noah had heard her, and suddenly he was filled with a fierce possessiveness. He knew then that he'd never be able to let her go. She was his to have, to hold and to protect. All he had to do was convince her that she belonged to him.

6

NOAH PURPOSELY KEPT their conversation light as they munched on pizza and sipped wine. He found himself intrigued by the way Sirena's eyes brightened and her face became animated as she talked about Barrington Foundation, and he could appreciate her feelings toward her business. He knew what it was like to take an idea, realize it and mold it to meet your dreams.

When she dropped some tomato sauce on her dress and glanced down at it in vexation, he chuckled. "Your cleaning bill must cost you a fortune."

"Normally, I'm very neat," Sirena muttered as she dabbed at the stain with her napkin, knowing that a good part of her sudden clumsiness had to do with Noah.

He was the only person she'd ever known who listened to her so completely. His eyes were always riveted on her face. His body was always leaning toward her, as if every word she spoke was so important he didn't want to chance missing one of them.

The problem was, his attention made her more aware of the blue of his eyes. The strength of his jaw. The way he smiled. The way he laughed. The coiled muscles beneath his clothes, and the unspoken promise of what it would be like to be held in his arms. She sighed inwardly, acknowledging that that promise was not given in vain.

"I've talked about myself long enough," she told him, deciding it was time to distract herself from his many charms. "Tell me about your business."

"Sure," Noah said as he leaned back in the booth. "What do you want to know?"

"The name would be a good place to start."

"Noah's Ark. Our motto is that we can give you the perfect match for all your business needs."

"I like it," Sirena said with a delighted laugh.

"In that case you should let me do a little digging into Barrington Foundation to see what we have to offer you," he said casually. Since he'd already set up his business affairs so that he could spend the majority of his time with her, he had every intention of accompanying her to work. He knew she'd be more amenable to the situation if she thought he was doing it for business reasons rather than personal ones.

"Drumming up business?"

He shrugged nonchalantly. "I never pass up the opportunity to drum up business. Besides, I'd like to see how you're handling your records. You're involved in so many activities that it must be difficult to keep up with everything. If we don't have software to fit your needs, I can always design something for you that will. What do you say?"

Sirena eyed him for a long moment, sensing that there was more going on here than a simple business proposition. But despite the little nagging voice inside that urged caution, her business concerns overrode her personal wariness. She'd known for several months that the foundation's records and retrieval system needed to be updated and expanded. She just hadn't gotten around to hiring a consultant to analyze the problem.

She took a sip of her wine before saying, "I suppose it wouldn't hurt if you sent someone from your office to do an analysis. How much do you charge?"

"For nonprofit organizations, nothing," he answered. "And I'll be doing the analysis."

That announcement made Sirena frown. "Why?"

"Because it's good public relations to waive a consulting fee for businesses involved in charitable works," he answered with deliberate obtuseness.

"That wasn't what I was asking, and you know it," Sirena told him, her frown deepening.

He widened his eyes in mock innocence. "It wasn't?"

"Noah."

He grinned at her warning tone. "All right. I'll be doing the analysis because I want to make sure that you get the best. It's the least I can do for my wife."

There were those two words again—*my wife*. The more he used them, the more comfortable Sirena felt with them, and that admission made her very uncomfortable. She knew she'd be foolish to even expect anything more than a mending of their fences, so to speak. As she'd told him the night he showed up on the mansion's doorstep, they were incompatible. Even if they were able to maintain a truce long enough to resolve their past, their tempers were too volatile to ever let them build anything permanent.

"I wish you wouldn't call me your wife," she said, her expression chastising. "We both know it isn't true. For all practical purposes, we're divorced."

Noah's temper began to stir, and he twirled his empty wineglass between his fingers as he forced himself to be calm. "Every judge in Pennsylvania would disagree with you," he finally said.

"Well, they'd be wrong," Sirena responded, her own temper beginning to stir.

"Maybe." Noah regarded her assessingly for a long time before asking, "Are you really serious about the old coot?"

"Would you please stop calling Jonathan an old coot?" Sirena stated irritably. "He's only forty-one, Noah. That hardly constitutes old age."

"And you're only twenty-six. Fifteen years is one hell of an age difference. If you had kids, he'd be pushing it to throw a football."

"I don't consider throwing a football the number-one priority for fatherhood, Noah."

"I was raised by an older father, Sirena. Believe me, when you're a kid, throwing a football, or a baseball or any other kind of ball with your father is important to you."

"Maybe Jonathan and I will have girls," she taunted, not about to inform him that she and Jonathan had parted ways the same day he and Noah had encountered each other. She had a feeling he'd use the information against her somehow.

Noah's eyes narrowed. "Then you are serious."

She shrugged and then blinked at him in disbelief when he asked, "How is he in the sack?"

"That question is positively uncouth and no gentleman would ever ask it," Sirena stated haughtily.

Noah leaned forward and rested his forearms on the table. "I never claimed to be couth or a gentleman. Is he good in bed?"

"I never kiss and tell," she snapped.

"Which means he isn't," Noah responded in satisfaction. He grinned when Sirena glared at him. "If you aren't going to think of your kids, you need to think of yourself, Sirena. You're too passionate a woman to tie yourself down with a man who can't—"

"That's enough," Sirena interrupted angrily. "Pay the check and take me back to the foundation. I'm driving myself home."

"Ah, I hit a sore spot."

"You did not hit a sore spot. I am simply not going to sit here and let you talk about my love life."

His grin widened when her glare became deadly. "You are so damn sexy when you're mad. It makes me want to throw you right down on the floor and . . ."

Sirena, finding herself wrestling with that familiar wave of half anger and half desire that he always seemed to incite within her, rose from her chair and walked purposefully toward the door. She knew that Noah couldn't possibly follow until he'd taken care of the check, and it was only about six blocks to the foundation. She could walk it in no time, but she hesitated when she stepped outside and eyed the dark streets surrounding her. This wasn't the best neighborhood for a woman to be on foot alone at night.

The choice was taken out of her hands when Noah exited. She hadn't been outside more than a few seconds, which meant he'd probably tossed a handful of bills onto the table. Sirena was wondering if the waitress was blessing him or cursing him over her tip as he grabbed Sirena's arm and began leading her toward his car.

Though he didn't say anything, she could feel his anger in his tight but gentle grip, and she steeled herself for battle. No matter what happened, she had to maintain control over the situation. But her body was already humming in anticipation of a confrontation and the memory of where it could lead. She gritted her teeth and firmly informed her libido that it was not going to have its way.

When they reached the car, he unlocked the passenger door. But instead of opening it, he turned her toward him and stated in clipped words, "Don't you ever walk out on me like that again."

Sirena's temper automatically flared at the dictatorial order. "I'll do whatever I want, and you can—"

Noah had had enough. Damn the woman anyway! She was his wife, and knowing that she'd been sleeping with another man was enough to provoke him to thoughts of murder. She belonged to him, and he was going to prove it to her right here and now.

He jerked her into his arms and sealed his mouth over hers, cutting off her protest. When she struggled against him, he merely tightened his hold on her. When she nipped at his tongue as he tried to thrust it into her mouth, he caught her hair in one of his hands and tangled his fingers in it until she was forced to give in or cause herself pain.

"That's it, mermaid. Sing for me," he crooned when she gave up the fight and leaned against him until he could feel every valley and curve of her soft body pressed against him and her lips moved hungrily against his.

Satisfied that he'd brought her to heel, he released his hold on her hair and let his hand glide down her spine. He groaned as he cupped her buttocks and began to lift her into the cradle of his thighs, but before he could complete the action Sirena braced her hands against his chest and shoved.

"What the hell!" Noah exclaimed in surprise as he stumbled half a dozen steps backward.

Sirena perched her hands on her hips and glowered at him. She was so livid that she wanted to scream at the top of her lungs and was half tempted to do so, even if it would most likely summon the police.

"You haven't changed at all," she told him in a low voice that crackled with her anger. "You still think that if I won't do what you want, all you have to do is haul me off to bed until I become agreeable. Well, it doesn't work any longer,

Noah, and I swear that if you ever use your caveman tactics on me again, you'll regret it."

Noah stuffed his hands into his pants pockets and sauntered toward her while murmuring softly, dangerously, "That sounds like a dare if I ever heard one."

Sirena watched his approach with a mixture of fury and trepidation. Her first instinct was to turn on her heel and run, but she knew that she couldn't show any sign of weakness, because this was one battle she was determined to win.

When he stopped directly in front of her, Sirena defiantly raised her chin a notch and met his stormy gaze unflinchingly. For a long moment they simply stood staring at each other, and she was completely taken aback when Noah suddenly grinned.

He reached out and gently stroked one finger along her tense jawline. "Relax, mermaid. Even if you do bring out the caveman in me, I can control him." He opened the car door and urged her inside. "Let's get you home and into bed. You need a good night's sleep."

Sirena was so baffled by his easy capitulation that she forgot to remind him she wanted to go back for her car.

She became even more rattled when they arrived at the mansion and Noah fished a key to the front door from his pocket, calmly announcing, "Tabitha said Ben would be retiring early and we'd have to let ourselves in."

Sirena didn't have a key to the house, and Ben had never failed to be at the front door when she came home. It looked as if her guardian angel was handing her over to the wolf! What in the world was she going to do if Noah decided to pick up where they'd left off in the parking lot? She'd never find enough strength to ward him off a second time, particularly when there was a bed close at hand.

Seemingly unaware of her distress, Noah led her inside, locked the door behind them and guided her up the stairs. Outside her bedroom door Sirena once again steeled herself for battle, only to be thrown off balance when all Noah did was brush a knuckle beneath her right eye.

"Get some sleep, Sirena," he told her. "You're starting to look like a raccoon. I'll let you use the bathroom first."

Then he turned and walked away, leaving Sirena gazing after him in bewilderment. Thirty minutes ago he'd been ready to ravish her in a public parking lot, and now he was sounding like a father!

She really had fallen down the rabbit hole, she decided as she walked through her room and into the bath. She completed her nightly routine in record time and crawled into bed, certain she'd never be able to fall asleep. But the stress of the past few days had taken its toll, and she was out almost as soon as her head hit the pillow.

Noah, on the other hand, was standing on the long balcony that ran the length of Sirena's wing of the house. His body was burning with a heat that was sure to incinerate him, and every time he glanced toward the sliding glass doors leading into her room, he had to force himself not to check and see if they were open.

Unbelievably, he wanted her more now than he ever had before, and he knew it was because he was discovering that the poor little rich girl was more woman than he'd ever given her credit for being. When she'd shoved him away tonight and called him a caveman, he'd been furious. But despite the defiant tilt of her chin and the challenging determination in her eyes, his anger had fled, because he'd also seen her internal struggle with her own desire. She'd wanted him as badly as he'd wanted her, but pride had made her deny herself.

Pride was something Noah understood fully. He'd been raised in a family of old-fashioned men, with old-fashioned values and archaic notions of a woman's place in the world. But being a businessman had taught him that the world had changed, values had changed, and women had changed. The majority of them were no longer satisfied to be considered members of the fairer sex who wanted to be coddled, but demanded to be recognized as individuals with a right to their own autonomy.

Until Sirena came along, Noah had been able to comfortably separate women into those two categories. But Sirena was an odd combination of both the old world and the new. He admired her keen intelligence and savoir faire, but he'd always sensed that beneath her polished exterior was a vulnerability that cried out for protection. The old-fashioned man in him automatically responded to that silent cry.

After living in the Barrington mansion he was beginning to understand where that vulnerability was coming from. He'd seen the proof of the old axiom that money couldn't buy happiness. Tabitha had spent her life pining over a lost love. Ophelia was haunted by the violent loss of a child. Pamela was still an enigma, but intuition told him that she, too, had been touched by tragedy. He also understood that Sirena was being torn between the demands of three strong-willed women and her own struggle to find her identity. He decided that he didn't envy her.

Unable to resist the temptation any longer, he found himself drawn to the sliding glass doors leading into her room. To his surprise they were open, and he slipped through the heavy curtains and crept to her bed.

Her red hair was fanned out across her pillow. Her lashes were so long they nearly covered the shadows beneath her eyes. Her lips were parted sweetly, and one hand was tossed above her head, while the other clutched the covers at her chest.

He couldn't resist the urge to reach out and caress her silken tresses, which curled around his fingers with a life of their own. Nor could he resist the urge to drop a gentle kiss to her parted lips. She stirred, murmuring in her sleep, and he smiled as she nestled her soft cheek against his palm.

It took every ounce of self-control he had to make himself leave her, but he knew that in order for Sirena to accept the fact that they belonged together, she had to come to him on her own. Only then could they begin to rebuild what they should never have let be torn down in the first place.

When he crawled into bed a long time later, he released a weary sigh. Not even a cold shower had eased the desire raging inside him, and he sent a silent prayer heavenward that his mermaid would see the light before he found himself on his deathbed. He chuckled wryly as he envisioned the inscription on his tombstone: Here lies Noah Samson. He died from unrequited lust.

NO MATTER HOW HARD Sirena tried, she couldn't dismiss the crazy dream that had been teasing at her ever since she'd opened her eyes this morning. In it Noah had come to her during the night and kissed her.

The dream had seemed so real that she'd actually checked both her bedroom door and the connecting bathroom door to ensure that they were securely locked. After confirming that they were, she decided her subconscious had been working overtime, and dressed for work.

Downstairs, she went looking for Noah. He was in the dining room, having breakfast with her aunt and her mother.

"Good morning," he said cheerfully when he saw her. He immediately rose to his feet and pulled out the chair beside him for her to sit down. "How is my wife today?"

An involuntary and not unpleasant shiver crawled up her spine at that damn proprietary title he insisted on using. Then her attention was drawn to the white silk shirt that was molded to his massive chest, the neatly tailored black slacks that emphasized his narrow waist, taut hips and muscular thighs. Her stomach quivered.

"Running late," she told him briskly, determined to ignore her traitorous body. "Are you about ready to leave, or should I ask the chauffeur to take me to work?"

"I'm almost ready to leave," Noah responded as he studied her through narrowed eyes, sensing that her temper was looking for a reason to go on the rampage. He wondered why. "Why don't you have some breakfast while I finish eating?"

"I don't have time for breakfast," Sirena stated irritably. "I just said I'm running late."

"There's no reason to be rude, Sirena," her mother chided.

"It's all right, Pamela," Noah quickly interjected when he saw Sirena's lips tighten in anger. He knew that an explosion was a short fuse away. "I lived with Sirena long enough to know that morning is not her best time of the day. She has to be coaxed into a better mood."

Sirena's face flooded with color as her mother chuckled knowingly and Tabitha said innocently, "You'll have to teach us that trick, Noah. We've never been able to coax Sirena into a better mood."

Noah's eyes were glinting with devilry as he stared at Sirena. "I don't think my technique would work for you, Tabitha."

"Oh!" Tabitha gasped as realization dawned. Her blush was as dark as Sirena's when she glanced toward her niece and then quickly away. "I suppose it, uh, wouldn't. Sirena, I'll ask Mrs. Mullen to pack you a nice breakfast to take with you. It is the most important meal of the day, you know."

Before Sirena could refuse her aunt's offer of sustenance, Tabitha had risen and scurried through the swinging doors that led into the kitchen.

"I'll get my jacket and be right down," Noah stated as he walked out of the room, seemingly unaware that Sirena's deadly glare was burning holes in his back.

"He's quite a man," Pamela commented when he'd disappeared.

Sirena turned on her mother. "He's a rude, obnoxious boor, and you know it."

Pamela sipped at her coffee before saying, "Maybe he simply takes his cues from you. You didn't need to snap at him, Sirena. A simple 'No thank you, Noah, I don't have time for breakfast this morning,' would have sufficed."

"I can't believe this," Sirena muttered in frustration. "I'm your daughter, but you're taking his side. What kind of mother are you?"

"The normal kind." Pamela set her coffee cup down and dabbed at her lips with her napkin. Then she smiled at Sirena. "I like him, Sirena, and I think you like him a lot more than you're willing to admit."

"I can't stand him," Sirena objected strenuously. "He's a damn caveman. His answer to everything is sex."

"All the more reason to like him," Pamela replied. She laughed softly when Sirena gaped at her in dumbfounded disbelief. "Honey, when two people first get married, they have to do a lot of adjusting in order to learn how to live with each other. That means that they fight over the silliest little things, because it's the silly little things that are the most difficult to learn to live with. A marriage wouldn't survive the first month if a couple didn't have overactive hormones to get them through that adjustment period, and let's face it, making up can be a lot of fun."

"There's only one flaw in your theory," Sirena stated grimly. "Noah doesn't make up in bed. He uses sex to make me bend to his will."

Pamela arched a disbelieving brow. "Sirena, I must know you far better than you know yourself. The only way sex would ever change your mind would be if you really didn't have intense feelings about the issue in the first place. You're far too strong-willed to ever be seduced into doing something that you don't want to do."

Pamela hesitated for a moment before she said, "I think your feelings for Noah are so deep that they frighten you, and believe it or not, I can identify with that. I felt the same way about your father, and I almost lost what turned out to be the best thing in my life because I was afraid of those feelings. Fear is a powerful motivator, Sirena. It's also our best weapon if we want to defeat ourselves."

Before Sirena could respond, Tabitha hurried back into the room with a small woven basket.

"Mrs. Mullen put in some of those muffins that Noah likes so well," her aunt gushed as she thrust the basket into Sirena's hands.

Sirena stared down at the basket while experiencing a strange pang of jealousy. It wasn't right that her aunt and the cook should know what muffins Noah liked, when she was married to the man and didn't know herself. She made a vow right then and there that from now on she'd be having breakfast with her husband.

NOAH FELT LIKE the proverbial cat on a hot tin roof when he came downstairs to drive Sirena to work. He expected her to still be in a snit. Instead, he found her inordinately calm, and the assessing way she kept staring at him had him wanting to check his tie for food stains.

"Something wrong?" he finally asked as he eased his car onto the interstate ramp that led to Barrington Foundation.

"No," Sirena answered.

Her simple response only heightened his uneasiness, and he risked a glance toward her. She smiled, which made him all the more nervous. What wicked machinations was she dreaming up to get even with him for that little scene in the dining room?

He cleared his throat uncomfortably. "I owe you an apology for this morning, Sirena. I shouldn't have teased you like that in front of your family."

She shrugged dismissively. "I deserved it. I was unnecessarily rude."

Noah began to go into a panic. "Not really. Morning isn't your best time of the day, and I should have shown some consideration."

"Yes, you should have," she agreed. "But, then again, I shouldn't have snarled at you in front of my family. I'll accept your apology if you'll accept mine."

Noah didn't speak until they arrived at Barrington Foundation. After he turned off the ignition, he turned to her and said, "Come on, Sirena. Yell at me and get it over with. I don't want to spend all day waiting for the ax to fall."

REWARD! Free Books! Free Gifts!

PLAY HARLEQUIN'S

LUCKY

CARNIVAL WHEEL

SCRATCH-OFF GAME

SCRATCH OFF HERE

FIND OUT IF YOU CAN GET

FREE BOOKS AND A SURPRISE GIFT!

PLAY THE
LUCKY
CARNIVAL WHEEL

scratch-off game
and get as many as
SIX FREE GIFTS...

HOW TO PLAY:

1. With a coin, carefully scratch off the silver area at right. Then check your number against the chart below it to find out which gifts you're eligible to receive.

2. You'll receive brand-new Harlequin Temptation® novels and possibly other gifts—ABSOLUTELY FREE! Send back this card and we'll promptly send you the free books and gifts you qualify for!

3. We're betting you'll want more of these heartwarming romances, so unless you tell us otherwise, every month we'll send you 4 more wonderful novels to read and enjoy. Always delivered right to your home. And always at a discount off the cover price!

4. Your satisfaction is guaranteed! You may return any shipment of books and cancel at any time. The Free Books and Gifts remain yours to keep!

NO COST! NO RISK!
NO OBLIGATION TO BUY!

FREE! 20K GOLD ELECTROPLATED CHAIN!

You'll love this 20K gold electroplated chain! The necklace is finely crafted with 160 double-soldered links, and is electroplate finished in genuine 20K gold. It's nearly ⅛" wide, fully 20" long—and has the look and feel of the real thing. "Glamorous" is the perfect word for it, and it can be yours FREE when you play the "LUCKY CARNIVAL WHEEL" scratch-off game!

More Good News For Members Only!

When you join the Harlequin Reader Service®, you'll receive 4 heartwarming romance novels each month delivered to your home at the members-only low discount price. You'll also get additional free gifts from time to time as well as our newsletter. It's ''Heart to Heart''—our members' privileged look at upcoming books and profiles of our most popular authors!

Sirena gave an innocent bat of her lashes. "I'm not going to yell at you, and there isn't any ax waiting to fall."

Noah scowled. "You're really starting to make me nervous, mermaid. We both know that you're all fire and brimstone, not sweetness and light. What kind of game are you playing?"

"I'm not playing any game," she answered. "I've decided to turn over a new leaf. From now on Sirena Angelica Barrington is going to be the most placid woman you've ever met."

"It's Sirena Angelica Barrington Samson," Noah corrected with another scowl.

Her lips twitched. "Of course. Forgive me for forgetting. Shall we go inside?"

Noah continued to stare at her with mistrust, but when she continued to smile sweetly at him, he finally gave up. With a muffled curse, he climbed out of the car and rounded it, deciding that she couldn't have found a better way to torment him if she'd tried.

When he opened the door and helped her out, she said, "Thanks," and began to sashay up the walk ahead of him.

Noah followed, unable to keep his eyes off the pencil-thin skirt that clung to her delightful derriere, and the provocative slit up the back that gave him more than a passing glance of thigh.

"That skirt is cut too high in the back for a day at the office," he grumbled when he hurried to open the front door for her.

"Really?" she questioned as she gave another innocent bat of her lashes. "Thank you for telling me, Noah. I'll make sure that I don't wear it to the office again. After all, it's very important that I appear professional."

Noah bit his inner cheek to keep from growling at her cheerful acceptance of his criticism.

Margie and Rufus the tiger were already at the front desk as they entered the reception area, and Sirena said, "Though I know you and Noah have met, Margie, I should make some formal introductions. This is Noah Samson, my husband. Noah, this is Margie Swenson, my right arm."

Before either could acknowledge the introductions, Sirena continued with, "Margie, Noah is going to be looking at our computer system to see if he can help us come up with a better way to handle our records. He can use the empty office in the back. Show him anything he wants to see, and introduce him to the rest of the staff. Everyone should feel free to tell him what they think would make their lives easier."

She turned to Noah. "I'll leave you in Margie's capable hands, but I'll be in my office if you need anything. Also, Mrs. Mullen packed some of those muffins you like so well. When you're ready for a break, they'll be waiting."

She started to walk away, but snapped her fingers and turned back to face him. "I just remembered what I forgot."

"What's that?" Noah inquired suspiciously.

"Your good-morning kiss," she responded brightly.

Since her three-inch heels nearly brought her to eye level with him, she only had to lean forward to brush her lips across his. The action was so light and so swift that it made Noah gulp. He'd never experienced anything so provocative.

"See you later," she murmured huskily.

"Yeah," he rasped.

"Gosh, I've never seen Sirena in such a good mood before noon," Margie commented as Sirena walked away and Rufus fell into step beside her.

"I know," Noah muttered as he watched her stroke the tiger's head before entering her office and closing the door. "It's damn scary."

7

NOAH NEVER DID come for his snack, and it was nearly noon when Sirena went looking for him. She stood in the doorway of the small office where Margie had stationed him. He was so absorbed in the stack of files in front of him that he didn't notice her, which gave Sirena a chance to study him surreptitiously.

She was surprised to see him wearing glasses. She also noted that they weren't sporty, fashionable frames, but sturdy, old-fashioned ones that suited his rugged, rakish face to perfection. His nose suddenly twitched and he glanced up at her.

"I thought I smelled company," he said with a grin as he leaned back in his chair, pushed the glasses to the top of his head and stretched.

Sirena chuckled as she walked into the room. "I hope that was a comment on my perfume and not my deodorant."

"It was the perfume," he assured. "You always smell good."

"Oh, I don't know about that," Sirena responded with a wry smile. "I remember a day not too long ago that I had a distinct barnyard scent."

"Believe me, Sirena, even chicken smells good on you," he said gallantly.

"You'd better be careful, Noah, or you're going to turn my head." She stopped at the side of his desk and eyed the stack of files. "I was going to see if you'd like to go to lunch, but it looks as if you're bogged down."

"A consultant is never bogged down, mermaid. Especially one who's working gratis. That also means you get to pay for lunch."

Though his words were nothing more than a small, innocuous comment that Sirena might have heard from any businessman, letting her pay for lunch was not the Noah she'd known two years ago.

"I suppose I can afford to pay for lunch."

"Great." He laid the files aside and tossed his glasses on top of them. "Where are we going to eat?"

"That's going to be my surprise."

He regarded her suspiciously as he rose to his feet. "Why do I get the feeling that the ax is about to fall?"

She simply smiled and asked, "When did you start wearing glasses?"

"Sixth grade. I only need them for reading."

"How come I never saw you wear them when we lived together?" she asked in surprise.

A grin immediately sprang to his lips, and he reached out to run his finger down her nose. "Honey, the last thing on my mind two years ago was reading."

Sirena silently cursed the blush she felt flooding her cheeks. "I suppose I should have seen that one coming."

"I suppose you should have," he murmured as he straightened a lock of hair that lay tangled on her shoulder. Then he brushed the back of his thumb across one of her heated cheeks. "I love the way you blush. It makes you look like a beautiful ripe peach. Did you know that your entire body blushes when you're turned on? It makes me want to gobble you right up."

"Noah!" The chastisement was actually more of a breathless exclamation of excitement, and she couldn't deny the tremor of longing that stirred in the pit of her stomach. "You shouldn't talk like that," she said more firmly. "Someone might hear you."

"So?" he asked as he bravely drew her into his arms and cradled her against his chest. He caught her chin and tilted her face upward. "You're my wife. I'm allowed to talk sexy to you."

"I wish you wouldn't."

"I know." He couldn't take his eyes off her enticing mouth. That fleeting half kiss she'd given him this morning had left his lips burning, and he needed a little balm to soothe them. "I want to kiss you, mermaid," he told her huskily. "But if I do, will I end up singing soprano for the rest of my life?"

Sirena had to swallow back a moan as the longing in her stomach shot downward and spread into her thighs, making them quiver. She knew she should pull away from him immediately, but all morning she'd been mulling over her mother's words, and she'd come to the conclusion that her mother was right. Noah could never seduce her into doing something she didn't want to do, and why should she deny herself the pleasure of his kisses?

Feeling reckless, she wrapped her arms around his neck, tilted her head to the side and puckered her lips invitingly.

Noah sucked in a deep breath and held it for a count of ten to keep from crushing her to him. Then he released it and lowered his lips to hers.

To Sirena's utter disbelief, it was the sexiest kiss she'd ever shared with him. Up until now, they'd always come together with a fiery passion, each trying to gain control over the other. But this time, Noah's lips were gentle and coaxing and ultimately more seductive.

She thought she'd die from the exquisite torture as he teased her with small fleeting kisses. When he nibbled on her lower lip, she automatically parted her lips to grant his tongue entrance, but he ignored the invitation as he nibbled his way to one corner of her mouth, and then back across the full length of her bottom lip to the other corner.

"Noah." His name came out as a plea, and she snuggled closer against him, moaning softly as he leaned back against the desk and drew her between his thighs. The proof of his desire made her knees go weak, and she knew she would have fallen if he hadn't chosen that moment to tighten his hold around her.

Noah was certain that at any moment he was going to go up in smoke, but he couldn't think of a better way to go. Sirena had never been so pliant in his arms, and it filled him with a passion that went beyond the physical. It touched him in places deep inside that had never been touched before, and he knew that when he finally made love to her again, this was the way he wanted it to be. Sweet and gentle and filled with tenderness.

Regretfully, he also knew he had to end the kiss before he lost all control and took her right there on the floor.

He smiled when she whimpered in protest as he ended the kiss, and he rested his cheek against her hair as she buried her face on his shoulder. Soothingly, he stroked her back and was amazed to find that as her body relaxed, his relaxed in mutual accord. He discovered that the sensation of being so attuned to her was nearly as satisfying as making love with her.

It was a long time before Sirena found the courage to raise her head, positive she'd see the gleam of male satisfaction in Noah's eyes. To her surprise, he smiled at her with a shy tenderness that tugged at her heart.

"I don't know what to say," she whispered in confusion.

He lifted her hand to his lips, pressing a kiss to her knuckles. "Sometimes words aren't necessary, mermaid. Besides, I'm hungry, and I believe my wife invited me to lunch. Is her invitation still open?"

Sirena nodded before sheepishly saying, "It's still open. However, I should warn you that we're going to be dining in one of the foundation's soup kitchens."

Noah blinked in astonishment. "You're going to eat in a soup kitchen?"

"Sure. I do it all the time. I drop in unannounced to try the food and make sure that the foundation's getting its money's worth. A soup kitchen is the perfect kind of operation to invite graft. So far we haven't had any problems, but I like to keep everyone on their toes. It also gives me an opportunity to talk directly to people who are on the streets, so I can be aware of any new problems arising."

Noah wasn't sure he liked the idea of Sirena visiting soup kitchens, or talking to street people for that matter, but he decided to reserve his opinion until he'd seen firsthand what was going on.

"Well, I've always been in favor of new experiences," he told her. "Lead the way."

AS WAS BECOMING THE NORM, Noah once again found himself discovering that Sirena was not the shallow woman he'd perceived her to be. She should have looked incongruous in the shabby but immaculately clean building that housed one of the foundation's four soup kitchens from Harrisburg to Lancaster. Instead, she looked perfectly at home as she went through the line, chatting with staff and bedraggled customers, while filling her tray with a bowl of the plain but hearty meat and vegetable stew, a hot dinner roll, a piece of fresh fruit and a glass of milk. It was only when she walked to one of the long tables and sat down next to a huge, ugly man who had ex-murderer written all over him that Noah's amazed approval turned to tacit disapproval.

As he walked toward the table to join her, he automatically sized up the giant Sirena had engaged in conversation. Though the man clearly outmatched him in height and weight, Noah decided he could take him with a little quick maneuvering, and he blessed his grandfather, who'd introduced him to blacksmithing at an early age. The hobby had allowed him to build up a pair of biceps that could deliver a tried and true knockout punch, though it had been a very long time since he'd had to use it. He also decided that after today, Sirena's soup kitchen visits were over.

"Oh, there you are, Noah," Sirena said when he sat down beside her. "I'd like you to meet John. John, this is my husband, Noah."

"John," Noah said with a short nod.

John nodded back, but didn't say anything.

Sirena, blissfully unaware of Noah's darkening mood, said, "John helped me out of a spot of trouble a few months back."

"A spot of trouble?" Noah repeated as his hand tightened around the soupspoon in his hand. "Just what is a *spot* of trouble?"

"Muggers," John said in a growling whisper, which Noah suspected was the result of a damaged larynx.

"Muggers!" Noah exclaimed lowly and dangerously.

"Oh, they weren't really muggers," Sirena said in exasperation. "They were simply a couple of rowdy kids."

Noah met John's small black eyes, and the silent communication they exchanged told him that Sirena was either making light of the situation or was simply too naive to realize that she'd been in real danger. He had the distinct feeling it was the latter, which didn't improve his flaring temper.

"Anyway," Sirena continued after taking a bite of her stew, having missed the silent male exchange, "John came out of the shadows and those two boys took off so fast they were no more than a blur."

"I can imagine," Noah stated tightly. "Just where did you encounter these rowdy kids?"

"Down by the train yard."

"At night," John added disapprovingly.

"Dammit, Sirena, what where you doing in the train yard at night?" Noah demanded.

She glanced up at him and frowned at the censorious note in his voice. "I wasn't in the train yard. I was by it, and I was looking for someone."

"By yourself. At night."

"Yes, by myself. At night." She stared at him challengingly. "I can take care of myself, Noah. I've had self-defense classes."

John choked on his roll.

Noah closed his eyes and rubbed the base of his palm against the bridge of his nose.

"Sirena," he said as he reopened his eyes and scowled at her. "The purpose of a self-defense class is to give you an edge if you happen to stumble into trouble. You aren't supposed to go looking for it."

"I wasn't looking for trouble. I was looking for a runaway."

"Down by the train yard at night."

"Yes, down by the train yard at night," she said with an irritated sigh. "Now that we've clearly established the where and the when, would you like to know the why?"

Noah couldn't help it. He had to grin at her aggravated expression. "All right, Sirena. Why?"

"I was told that there was a pregnant runaway living in a condemned building down by the rail yard. It was twenty degrees outside, and it was predicted that the temperature was going to drop below zero. I wasn't about to leave a pregnant girl in a rat hole without heat. It was lucky that I showed up, because when John and I found her, she was in labor. I had to deliver the baby. All by myself," she added as she shot an amused look at John. "Gentle John, here, took one look at her and fainted dead away."

Noah couldn't decide which he found more unbelievable. Sirena delivering a baby in a condemned building, or John the behemoth fainting dead away at the sight of a woman in labor.

"You delivered a baby?" When Sirena nodded, he asked, "Where did you learn how to do that?"

Sirena gave him a self-complacent smile. "I'm a woman, Noah. Some things you just know by instinct."

John's chuckle sounded eerily like Rufus's purr.

Noah shook his head in chagrin. "So what happened to mother and baby?"

Sirena turned toward the serving line and nodded toward the girl with a sleeping baby in a pack on her back, who'd dished up their stew. "They're right over there. Lori works here part-time and goes to school at night. Anne and George," she said, naming the couple who ran the soup kitchen for the foundation, "have taken her in for now. When she gets her general equivalency diploma she's going to work at the foundation's day-care center."

Noah shook his head again, and though he wanted to rail at Sirena for putting herself in danger, he also appreciated her noble deed. He decided to let the situation ride for now and took a bite of the stew, discovering that it tasted as good as it looked.

As Sirena continued to chat with John, Noah's eyes drifted around the room. Studying the crowd, he noted that the ages ranged from infants to the very old. He knew many of the elderly had been bussed there, because he'd seen the bus outside and Sirena had told him that they serviced many elderly people on fixed incomes who were struggling to survive.

"Noah, is something wrong?" Sirena asked in concern when John left the table and she glanced at Noah. There was a strange, almost heart-wrenching expression on his face.

"Yes," he said as he glanced toward her. "I hate poverty."

"So do I," she said quietly.

"But you don't know what it's like to live like this." He glanced around the room again. "You don't know what it's like to go to school hungry, or to be wearing hand-me-downs that are either too large or too small. You don't know how humiliating it is to have adults staring at you with the same sympathetic expressions they'd give a stray dog and kids bullying you because you don't fit in."

"And you do."

It was an observation, not a question, and Noah nodded. "I do."

"Would you tell me about it?"

He looked at her then, half expecting to see that sympathetic expression that he'd learned to despise as a child— the one he'd sworn he'd never see aimed his way again. But Sirena's eyes were clear and direct, and her expression was neutral.

"It's not a very pretty story, mermaid."

"Life rarely is pretty," she responded. When he didn't say anything, she went on, "You know, the only member of your family that you ever told me about was your grandfather. I don't know if your parents are alive, or if you have brothers and sisters. Every time I asked about your family, you'd change the subject. Why, Noah?"

He shrugged and stirred the stew in his bowl. "My family isn't exactly in your league, Sirena."

"You're embarrassed by your family?" she questioned in horrified disbelief.

Noah's head snapped toward her and anger flared into his eyes. "No, I'm not embarrassed by them. I love them very deeply. So deeply that I'd never put them into a position where they might get their feelings hurt."

"And you thought I'd hurt their feelings." Again, it wasn't a question, but a statement. Tears sprang into Sirena's eyes and she gave a miserable shake of her head. "I know you thought I was shallow, but I didn't know you also thought I was cruel."

Her tears caused Noah's heart to ache, and he reached for her hand. "Sirena . . ."

But she pulled away from him and rose to her feet. "Please excuse me. I need to take care of some business."

Noah inwardly cursed as he watched her walk away, her spine stiff and proud. When she disappeared through the door leading into the kitchen, he wanted to slam his fist down on the table. She'd completely misinterpreted his words.

He'd never believed that she was cruel, nor had he ever thought that she'd purposely hurt his family's feelings. But he knew the Samson pride well enough to predict how they would have reacted to his poor little rich girl. All of them would have been intimidated. In self-protection, his father and older brothers would have treated her with disdain. His mother and older sisters would have withdrawn from her in acute shyness. Noah also knew himself well enough to understand that he would have responded defensively and taken it out on all of them, including Sirena. Thus, he'd kept them apart.

He took a healthy swing of his iced tea, wishing it was Scotch as he recalled the old proverb, "Pride goeth before destruction, and an haughty spirit before a fall." Damn, if the scribe hadn't had him in mind when he'd written that one.

"Hi," a young voice said, and Noah glanced up to see Sirena's runaway teenager. The girl had removed the sleeping baby from the backpack and was holding it in her arms as she settled across the table from him. "Are you really Sirena's husband?"

"Yes," Noah said, automatically returning her smile. "And you're Lori."

The girl nodded before laying the baby on the table. "This is Michael. He's four months old today."

"He's a beautiful baby," Noah said sincerely as he tentatively reached out and stroked the infant's tiny fingers. "He looks awfully small for four months."

"He was premature," Lori said as she fussed at the baby's lightweight blanket. "If it wasn't for Sirena, I'm not sure he'd even be alive."

"She told me she delivered him."

"Yeah. Not only that, she hired the best doctors in the country to take care of him. His lungs weren't fully developed and it was touch and go for a while." She looked up at Noah, her eyes shining. "I'll never be able to pay Sirena back for all she's done for us."

"I have a feeling she doesn't want to be paid back," Noah replied, startled by how easily those words had come, but also convinced that they were true.

"That's what she says. She told me that being the best mother I can possibly be will be payment enough, but that doesn't seem like enough to me, know what I mean?"

"I think so."

Lori nodded and glanced away from him as she announced, "Sirena's out in the alley. I think she's crying."

Noah was instantly on his feet. "Where's the alley?"

"Through the kitchen and out the back door."

SIRENA CURSED INWARDLY when Noah's shoes appeared in her line of vision. She knew her cheeks were tearstained, and she wanted to tell him to go away and leave her alone. Instead, she curled her legs beneath her and leaned back against the building, refusing to speak or look at him.

"If you wanted to go on a picnic, why didn't you say so?" Noah stated lightly as he sat down beside her on the small plot of grass.

Sirena shrugged, knowing that she didn't dare trust her voice. His slur on her character had cut her more deeply than she would ever have thought possible, and the worst part was, she wasn't sure that she didn't deserve a part of it. She would never have purposely hurt anyone's feelings, but when she married him she was a spoiled little rich girl with no concept of life outside the walls of the Barrington mansion. It was very possible that she might have hurt his family without even realizing it.

She wanted to blame an overprotective and overindulgent environment for that failing, but the truth was she'd never bothered to look beyond the Barrington walls until she married Noah. During the short time she lived with him she'd learned that there was another side of life, and she'd envied him. She'd always had the money to buy whatever she wanted, but she'd never had true freedom.

She'd come to the conclusion that *rich* was simply a four-letter word for a complex form of slavery.

"I'm the youngest of nine children," Noah suddenly stated. "I was also a midlife surprise to my parents, who were dirt-poor farmers already financially taxed to feed the mouths they had.

"When I was seven," he continued, "my father was hurt in a farming accident that left him in a wheelchair, and my mother had to go to work. Every day that he watched her walk out the door he became more bitter, because the Samson men had always taken care of their women. My mother's skills were limited, which meant her salary was a pittance. Eventually they lost the farm. They were eligible for assistance but too proud to take advantage of it, so we went to live with my grandfather in Bedford."

Sirena, absorbed by his story, glanced toward him, forgetting her tearstained cheeks.

Noah reached out and gently traced the trail of a tear with his finger. "I spent my childhood and adolescence listening to my father lecture me on a man's role in the world. Pride was the key word, Sirena. A man was not a man unless he could stand on his own two feet and support his family. It may sound like an old-fashioned value to you, but it was an old-fashioned value that was drummed into me from the time I was born. My family could have never accepted the fact that I was married to a woman so wealthy that she didn't need me. Your money also scared the hell out of me."

"But why?" Sirena asked fervently. "Didn't you understand that all I had was also yours?"

He shook his head. "It could never be mine, mermaid, because I didn't earn it."

"I didn't earn it, either," she objected. "I was born into it. If one of your sisters had married a rich man, would your family have turned their back on her?"

"No," Noah answered honestly. "But it would have been different. My sisters are women."

"That's an unfair double standard, Noah."

"Yes, it is," he agreed reluctantly. "But I am what I am, Sirena. I might be able to soften, but I can't change my basic beliefs. I need to be needed. Two years ago, you didn't need me."

She stared at the crumbling brick of the building across the alley and said, "I did need you two years ago. I actually had something to look forward to when I opened my eyes each morning. I got to cook and to clean. I got to go to the grocery store and the Laundromat. Real people actually talked to me, instead of treating me as if I were some kind of visiting royalty. For the first time in my life I was truly happy."

"You've got to be joking!" Noah said with a bark of laughter.

She turned a solemn gaze on him. "Happiness is not something I'd ever joke about. I'd have given away my entire fortune to continue living in that tiny efficiency apartment with you."

He peered at her in confusion. "Then why did you leave?"

"You told me to leave."

"I was angry," he stated impatiently. "I'd told you to leave before and you hadn't. Why did you suddenly decide to take me literally?"

"Because your eyes told me that you'd gone beyond anger," she replied sadly. "When you told me to get out that morning you meant it, because at that moment you hated me."

Noah leaned his head back against the building as he
acknowledged the truth of her words. When he told her
to leave during that last battle, he had hated her. His
damnable pride had been wounded when she offered him
money, and no matter how hard his common sense had
fought against it, he'd been incapable of overcoming that
reaction. He'd kept seeing his father's despairing face as
he watched his wife leave for work each day, and the
thought of being even temporarily dependent on Sirena
had terrified him.

"Maybe I did hate you at that moment, but the feeling
didn't last more than a few hours. When I came home that
night and found you gone, I sat down and . . ."

"You sat down and what?" Sirena prodded.

"Cried," Noah answered as he stared at the building in
front of him. "I hadn't shed a tear since I was five years old,
but that night I sobbed like a baby."

"Oh, Noah," Sirena whispered as she reached out and
touched his cheek.

Noah turned his head toward her. "Don't cry, Sirena,"
he said hoarsely as he watched tears begin to slide down
her cheeks. "I can't stand to see you cry."

But Sirena couldn't stop, because his confession had
touched a chord inside her that forced her to face the truth.
She'd been madly in love with every chauvinistic bone in
Noah's body two years ago, and she was madly in love
with every one of them today. The trouble was, he was in
love with his Cynthia, and Sirena had caused him to lose
her. He had to truly hate her now.

"Sirena, stop it," Noah murmured when she began to
sob.

When his gentle order only made her cry harder, he
pulled her into his arms. She buried her face against his
shoulder, clinging to him desperately as he stroked her

back and her hair while whispering soothing platitudes in her ear.

"Sirena, please stop," Noah pleaded when nothing he said seemed to calm her. But his plea went unheeded, and Noah finally resorted to the only option he had left. He lifted her face and kissed her.

8

SIRENA'S TEARS BEGAN to ebb as Noah's lips moved over hers provocatively, irresistibly. She still clung to him, but it was no longer a lamentable embrace. It was an effort to communicate with her body what she could never tell him in words.

She gasped softly when Noah groaned and hauled her onto his lap. His hand settled over her breast, his thumb stroking its peak until her nipple hardened and ached with pleasure.

"Sirena, tell me to stop or I'm going to take you right here," he muttered against her lips.

But before she could utter a sound he kissed her again, and she was his to do with as he wished. When his hand shifted from her breast to her thigh, and he slid it beneath her skirt, she began to strain toward him in encouragement.

It was her turn to groan as he jerked his head back, leaving her lips feeling lonely and abandoned.

"Give me strength," he rasped harshly as he rested his head against the building and closed his eyes.

"I think," Sirena said taking a deep breath and praying for her own strength, "that we should go back inside."

Noah's eyes shot open and Sirena was startled by the rage glimmering in their depths. He settled his hands on her shoulders and gave her a hard shake as he said, "Dammit, Sirena, stop running away from me!"

"I'm not running away!" she exclaimed, her own temper flaring. "I'm simply trying to prevent a situation that we'll both end up regretting."

He jerked her to his chest and glared down into her wide, dismayed eyes. "Neither of us would regret that situation, and you know it. You want me as much as I want you."

"Yes," Sirena admitted angrily. "I do want you, but you're in love with another woman. She was standing by your side in that chapel, remember? You'd set up a seductive honeymoon retreat for her, remember? My word, your bed was covered with rose petals!"

The rage immediately drained from his eyes and was replaced with masculine conceit. He gave her a thousand-volt satyr's grin as he said, "You sound jealous."

"I am not jealous!" she denied ardently. "I'm being practical. I made you lose the woman you love and you're out to punish me for it. Well, Noah, I'm sorry, but I will not sleep with you so you can have your revenge."

"I'm not out for revenge, Sirena."

"Of course you are. Why else would you be here?"

"Wiggle your bottom and you'll find out," he drawled as his grin widened.

"That is not only disgusting, Noah, but it proves my point," she stated huffily.

"You're wrong on both counts, mermaid. It's not disgusting, but the truth. As far as your point goes, I have no reason to seek revenge because I was never in love with Cynthia."

"Of course you were. You were about to marry her!" Sirena argued.

"And you saved me from making the second biggest mistake of my life. I liked Cynthia, and I still like her for that matter, but I was not in love with her. Just like you're not in love with the old coot."

"Jonathan is not an old coot!" Sirena railed in frustration. "He's a wonderful man."

"Wonderful enough to make you quiver?" Noah asked as he stroked his hand from her waist to her breast. "Wonderful enough to make you ache with passion? Wonderful enough to—"

"Noah!" It was not only a demand for silence, but a plea for sanity, because his thumb was once again stroking her nipple, causing her womb to turn inside out.

"He isn't that wonderful, is he, Sirena?" Noah challenged seductively.

"Why are you doing this to me?" she questioned plaintively as she tried to shift away from his exploring hand, only to have him tighten his hold on her.

"Because what we have is special, Sirena."

"But you don't love me."

He shrugged, rejecting her words. "Actually, I don't know what name to give my feelings for you. You're the complete opposite of what I've always envisioned in a wife, but when I'm with you I feel more alive than I've ever felt with any other woman."

Sirena gave a resigned shake of her head. "So we're back to sex, aren't we?" Before he could respond, she said, "Passion eventually wanes, Noah, and as you said, I'm the opposite of what you want in a wife. We could never make a long-term relationship work, because once we settled down into a normal routine our differences would begin to drive us crazy."

"I agree that we couldn't have made it work two years ago," Noah responded. "Both of us needed to do a lot of growing up. But we've matured, Sirena, and I think we could learn to compromise on our differences."

"Oh, Noah, I don't know," Sirena murmured as she studied his face. He looked so serious, so resolute, and deep down inside she wanted to give in to him. But there was a deeper, more primitive need for self-protection. Noah had already broken her heart once. She didn't think she could survive the experience a second time.

Noah seemed to sense her reluctance, because he said, "You've given me a month. Why don't we spend that time finding out if we can become friends?"

"Friends?" Sirena repeated doubtfully. The word was definitely too tame for any relationship that she could ever envision between them. But as he continued to regard her, silently waiting for her answer, she also knew that she had to take a chance, because she was and would forever be in love with Noah Samson. If she couldn't have his love, she had to have his friendship. It would be the only way that she could keep track of him.

"All right, Noah," she agreed, albeit reluctantly. "Let's find out if we can be friends."

Noah released an inward sigh of relief. It had seemed to take her forever and a day to agree to his suggestion, but now that she had, he knew that they'd just taken a major step forward. He also knew that from this moment on he would have to exercise extreme patience, which would definitely be a test of his mettle, because he was not a patient man.

SIRENA HAD NEVER BEEN so dirty, nor had she ever had so much fun in her life. The two young men she was helping to rip out the foundation's old furnace and air-conditioning system were stand-up comics at night, and they'd had her laughing almost from the moment they arrived.

"Oh, please stop!" she begged when they told still another joke. "I can't take any more."

"Ah, come on, Ms Barrington," Darren, the youngest of the two men, cajoled. "We're on a roll."

"Her name is Mrs. Samson," a deep voice growled from behind her.

"Noah!" Sirena exclaimed, then spun around and watched Noah emerge from the shadows, Rufus at his heels. The big cat had taken a liking to Noah and dogged his steps, a fact that had dumbfounded Sirena. Because Rufus had been abused by a man, he'd always been cautious around males, and though Noah complained vociferously about his feline shadow, Sirena knew he was secretly pleased. On many occasions she'd seen him scratching Rufus's ears or murmuring to him when he didn't think anyone was looking.

"Geez, it's a tiger!" one of the young men yelled in fright.

"It's just Rufus," Sirena said as she glanced over her shoulder at the two workers, who were cowering against the back wall. "He's toothless, clawless, nearly blind and half-crippled with arthritis. He couldn't hurt you if he wanted to."

She watched Darren cautiously shift his eyes from Rufus to Noah. "Is the guy as safe as the tiger?" he asked warily.

Sirena glanced toward Noah, took note of his glower and released a disgruntled sigh. "The guy's my husband, and I assure you his growl is worse than his bite."

Noah arched a brow at her comment, his glower turning into a frown.

"My word, Sirena. You look like a chimney sweep."

"It's all the new rage," she quipped, patting her hair. "Coal dust on percale and denim. What do you think?"

"I think that you need a bath," Noah stated as he stepped forward, pulled his handkerchief out of his back pocket and began to wipe at her face. The white linen was instantly black, and he grumbled an inarticulate curse as he turned it over and continued his cleanup. "Why didn't you tell me you were having the furnace replaced today? I would have taken care of it for you."

Sirena automatically bristled. "The furnace isn't your problem, Noah. You're a consultant, remember?"

"I'm also a man, Sirena, and this is a man's job."

"You're walking a chauvinistic tightrope," she warned as her temper began to stir.

A muscle twitched along his jawline for a moment, and then he grinned. "Old habits are hard to break."

Sirena gave him a guarded look, skeptical of his easy submission. "What are you doing down here anyway?"

"Rufus was getting bored and wanted to go for a walk," Noah said, not about to tell her that he'd missed her and gone looking for her. He also wasn't about to confess that when he'd heard her laughing uninhibitedly with the two young men every bone in his body had burned with jealousy. She'd never laughed like that with him. "How much longer does he have to be locked up in this concrete prison?"

"Until the end of the week," Sirena answered as she automatically glanced toward the tiger in concern. "I'm sorry, Rufus," she murmured as she stroked his head. "I know you want to be free, but I want you to be healthy. You just have a few more days to go, so hang in there. Before you know it, you'll be back at the mansion chasing butterflies and bees."

"Don't be ridiculous," Noah muttered as he absently scratched Rufus's ears. "He's a tiger. He'll chase birds and rabbits. Don't try to turn him into a wimp, Sirena. An identity crisis like that could cause him irreparable psychological damage."

Sirena fought hard to control her twitching lips as she took note of the serious expression on Noah's face. "Well, I certainly wouldn't want to do that to him."

Noah, sensing the facetiousness of her words, regarded her suspiciously. But if she was making fun of him he decided to ignore it when she gave him a sweet smile. He also had to stuff his hands into his pants pockets to refrain from reaching out and sweeping her into his arms. Dirty and disheveled became her. She looked far more approachable and desirable than he'd ever seen her. But he'd vowed to maintain his distance, and maintain it he would.

It had been a week since their talk at the soup kitchen where they agreed to try being friends. At the time his suggestion had seemed perfectly reasonable. He'd figured that if Sirena was able to forget about their inauspicious past and concentrate on the present she'd be more receptive to the idea of their sharing a future. However, he hadn't foreseen how he'd respond to Sirena with her guard down. The water bill at the mansion had to have increased twofold already. By the end of the month it would probably set an all-time record for the state of Pennsylvania. He'd also discovered that a cold shower was highly overrated for its effects on the libido.

"I have to pay a visit to my office tomorrow," he told her. "I thought you might enjoy coming with me, so I checked with Margie and she said your calendar is free. I'll only need a few hours to take care of business, and I thought we might spend the remainder of the day at Gettysburg. What do you say?"

The word *no* instantly sprang to Sirena's lips, but as she stared up at him, she saw hopeful expectancy in his eyes and her refusal wouldn't come out. It was dangerous, she told herself. In the past week she'd found her defenses crumbling. When he first suggested they make an attempt to become friends, she'd been sure his motives were devious; however, it was now becoming evident he was sincere. Not once had he made any physical advances to her, which, to her chagrin, was beginning to irritate her.

On the other hand, she'd learned more about him in the past week than she'd thought possible. He'd been responsive to every one of her questions. She now knew that his favorite color was yellow, which she found intriguing, considering his volatile temper and propensity for dark moods. He loved black-cherry ice cream and was fascinated by Civil War battlegrounds. She'd been surprised to learn that it wasn't the actual war that attracted him, but a desire to understand the motivations behind a war that would turn father against son and brother against brother. It was a fact that he found inconceivable, and as he talked about it he'd provided Sirena with his biggest revelation of all. For Noah there was nothing in the world more sacred than family.

"I'd love to go with you tomorrow," she heard herself say, startled by her involuntary acceptance. But any remaining hesitation she might have had was swept away when he gave her a boyishly excited smile.

"Great. I'll see you later."

Sirena shook her head in amusement as she watched man and tiger walk away. Both gave the impression of power and danger, yet she was beginning to discover that they were both about as dangerous as pussycats.

NOAH COULDN'T MAKE head or tail of the account he was reviewing. All the financial records for the foundation had been logical up to this point and easily entered into the accounting software program he'd developed for his own

business. But this account made no sense. Its disbursements were erratic and generally for enormous amounts.
There didn't seem to be an opening balance, nor could he
find a running balance. Even the name of the account,
which was simply called BHA, was an enigma, as were the
tag names applied to the disbursements.

"Well, Rufus," Noah said to the tiger, "I suppose we'd
better go ask Margie to explain this account to us."

Rufus lumbered to his feet and fell into step beside
Noah, bumping his large head against Noah's hand as they
walked down the hall until Noah gave in and scratched his
ears.

"Well, if it isn't Pete and Re-Pete," Margie said with a
chuckle as she glanced up from the paperwork in front of
her, eyeing Noah and Rufus.

Noah gave her a mock glare as he once again scratched
the tiger's ears. He dropped into the chair beside her desk
and Rufus sprawled at his feet. "I won't even bother to respond to that. I do have my dignity, you know."

Margie laughed. "I wouldn't expect you to respond. So,
what's up?"

"I can't figure out this account. There's no rhyme or
reason to it." Noah handed Margie the computer printout
he'd been struggling with for the past hour.

She accepted the paperwork, glanced at it and grinned.
"Of course there's no rhyme or reason to it. This is Sirena's bleeding heart account."

"Bleeding heart account?" Noah repeated. "That's what
the BHA stands for?"

Margie's grin widened. "Yep. You see, we occasionally
have off-the-wall situations that really don't fit into the
foundation's services. Since Sirena is very careful to ensure that the foundations's charter is followed to the letter

so that we don't endanger our tax-free status, she pays for them out of her personal account.

"For instance," Margie continued as she leaned toward him and pointed at the first entry under the M's, MacBail. "Mrs. MacIntosh's son got arrested and she couldn't afford bail. Sirena gave it to her." She pointed to the next entry, MilBabe. "Mr. and Mrs. Miller are a sweet old couple on a poverty-level retirement pension. Their daughter lives in California and was about to give birth to their first grandchild. Also, her husband had just been laid off from his job. Sirena paid for the Millers to fly out to be with her and covered all of their daughter's hospital expenses when she delivered as well."

Noah studied the next entry. "Don't tell me. MooWed has to do with someone's wedding."

"You've got it," Margie said with another chuckle. "Deena Moore does some volunteer work here. She wanted a church wedding, but couldn't afford it. Sirena went through the ceiling when she heard Deena was getting married by a judge, and paid for the wedding."

"If Sirena pays out of her personal checking account, why do you keep a record of these people?" Noah inquired.

"Because I'm afraid that my softhearted employer is also a soft touch and would die before she'd ever ask for a receipt or a bill. She'd simply hand over a check for whatever amount they claimed they needed. Since I don't want to see her generosity abused I serve as the go-between."

"I see," Noah said as he frowned at the printout. Then he rose to his feet and crossed to the window. As he stared out at a humid, cloudy sky that threatened rain he asked, "Margie, do you think Sirena is trying to overcompensate for being wealthy?"

"Sometimes," Margie answered.

"Is it an obsession?" Noah asked next as he turned to face her.

She shook her head. "She has a true desire to help the less fortunate. There are, however, times when I think that desire is fueled by some need to prove something to herself, especially when it comes to this account."

"What makes you say that?" Noah asked, needing to hear the young woman's answer.

Margie gave an uncomfortable shrug of her shoulders. "It's just a feeling, Noah, and I can't really pinpoint a reason. But I do know that if you really want to hurt Sirena, all you have to do is intimate that she's being shallow or selfish. It's as if she needs this account to prove to herself that she isn't."

Noah's stomach twisted into a painful knot of guilt at Margie's words. Though he kept telling himself that his harsh accusations of two years ago weren't Sirena's prime motivator for her bleeding heart account, he couldn't quite convince himself that he was right. He retrieved the computer printout from Margie with a gruff "Thanks," and was out the door before she could respond.

Back in his office, he began to tally the entries in the account on the calculator. When he finally had a total, he looked at it and let out a low whistle.

He leaned back in his chair, eyeing the walloping figure with a mixture of feelings. He knew Sirena could afford the expense, but he couldn't allay the feeling that it was also guilt money and that he was the person who'd given birth to that guilt.

Rufus rested his head in Noah's lap, and he absently stroked the tiger as he gazed at the blank, off-white wall in front of him. His ears burned with his demeaning words of two years ago. Shallow, selfish and spoiled were some of his gentler criticisms. He wouldn't allow himself to actually face his more abasing ones, because he now understood that she'd never deserved any of them.

It was true that Sirena had changed—become more aware of the world surrounding her—and that she was doing her part to improve the quality of life for those less fortunate then she. But Noah also knew that if she'd really deserved his accusations, she would never have made those changes. She'd still be the same shallow, selfish and spoiled little rich girl that he'd so often accused her of being.

Never before had he been more aware of how pride could lower a man, for it was his own pride—his own lack of a feeling of self-worth—that had made him debase her. He'd done his best to strip away her self-esteem in order to elevate his. The realization made him furious with himself.

"Noah?" Sirena stepped into his office and came to an abrupt halt as he turned glowing, angry eyes on her. "I'm sorry," she said. "I didn't mean to interrupt you."

"Don't be silly," he stated gruffly. "I work for you, remember? You can interrupt whenever you want."

Sirena stared at him in confusion. The anger had already disappeared and had been replaced with an emotion that she couldn't quite interpret.

Nervously, she said, "I, uh, wondered if you could come down to the basement and give me some advice. They're having problems installing the new furnace, and I don't know what they're talking about. I thought you might understand, and . . ."

"Let's go," Noah said as he rose to his feet, feeling an inordinate amount of pleasure that she'd come looking for him when faced with a dilemma. "I don't know much about furnaces, but I think I know enough to understand if I'm being given a song and dance."

"Great," she said, obviously relieved. "It's all Greek to me."

Noah couldn't help but smile as he advanced on her. Her face was once again smudged with coal dust, and with her hair caught in a ponytail, she looked more like a little girl than a woman. He also understood at the moment that his feelings for Sirena ran much deeper than lust. He was falling in love with her.

"Come on, mermaid," he said as he wrapped an arm around her shoulders and led her to the elevator. "Let's go take care of your problem together."

Sirena stared up at him, feeling mystified, for she had the feeling that Noah was referring to more than her furnace.

9

IF SIRENA HAD BEEN ASKED to describe what she expected Noah's offices to look like, she would have predicted austere professionalism. Thus, she was astonished when Noah pulled into the parking lot of a whimsical bright yellow building, its front renovated to resemble the bow of a ship, complete with portholes instead of windows.

"Noah, it's fabulous!" Sirena declared with enthusiasm.

"I like it," Noah said, unable to pull his gaze away from her face when she turned to look at him. She'd caught her shoulder-length red hair into a soft bun at the back of her neck, and wispy tendrils had escaped to frame her face and trail down her neck, giving her a fragile, dreamy look. The hairstyle also emphasized the delicacy of her bone structure and the enormous width of her eyes, which were sparkling with such vivacity that he found himself drowning in their depths. He couldn't stop himself from reaching out and touching the sprinkle of freckles that dusted her nose. "You're very beautiful, did you know that?"

"I'm very average," she demurred.

"Mermaid, I assure you that no one would ever describe you as average," he responded huskily.

Sirena dropped her gaze to her hands, which were nervously linked together in her lap. The look in Noah's eyes and the sincerity in his voice had sent a pang of yearning flowing through her. She kept telling herself that he was merely being polite. After all, she looked in the mirror every day of her life. The problem was, Noah did make her feel beautiful.

She jumped when his hand caught her chin, and he raised her head so that she was forced to look at him. He didn't speak, and his silence only increased her tension as he scrutinized her through a shield of long black lashes.

"You really don't know, do you?" he finally said in thoughtful amazement. Before she could come up with any semblance of an answer to his confusing comment, he climbed out of the car and rounded it. As he took her hand and helped her out of the car, he said, "Come on, mermaid. It's time for the grand tour."

Sirena's self-consciousness evaporated as he led her into the building, still tightly clasping her hand. She let out a delighted laugh as her gaze flew around the interior. The walls had been painted with a marvelous mural of an ark being filled with computer technology. Animated computer monitors were marching hand in hand up the plank. Floppy disks were already on board and were leaning over the railing, their cartoon hands gesturing in encouragement. Boxes of computer paper were dashing across the ground, with their lids lifted high against splattering raindrops. There were computer boards and instruction manuals and every conceivable computer accessory in various stages of boarding the ark.

"Do you like it?" Noah asked.

"I adore it," Sirena answered as she continued to scan the room, a wide grin on her face.

"You don't find it offensive?"

"Of course not," Sirena said, glancing toward him in surprise. "Why would I find it offensive?"

He gave an uncertain shrug of his shoulders. "Some people might think I was making fun of the biblical story, but that wasn't my intention."

Sirena, understanding his concern, restudied the scenes with a critical eye, but she couldn't find any reason for even the most devout to be offended by the mural; it wasn't done with a satirical overtone.

"It's done in very good taste," she told him as she gave his hand a reassuring squeeze. She was even more surprised by his sigh of relief.

"I'm glad you approve. Let's introduce you to everyone."

Noah spent the next ten minutes introducing Sirena to his staff, which totaled ten. Half of them ran the retail side of his business, which dealt with the general population who owned home-based personal computers. The other half dealt with the business needs of the community, and it was with this group that Noah conferred, leaving Sirena to explore the store.

It soon became apparent that his staff were curious about her, and a few of them even looked familiar to her. They'd probably been at Noah's aborted wedding, she realized with a flood of embarrassment as she recalled the details of that horrible scene.

When Steve Noble, one of the salesman, offered her a cup of coffee, Sirena eagerly agreed and followed him into the employees' lounge, figuring it would be easier to cope with one pair of curious eyes than five.

"This is a very nice lounge," she said, surveying the room, which contained a small kitchen area, complete with microwave oven, and a grouping of comfortable-looking, overstuffed chairs. There was also a television, a VCR and an expensive-looking stereo system.

Steve nodded as he poured her a cup of coffee. "Noah's given us all the comforts of home. It's one of the reasons he has such low personnel turnover. Sugar and cream?"

"Black." Sirena took the offered cup and settled into one of the chairs.

When he joined her a moment later, he said, "I want to apologize for my co-workers. They didn't mean to make you feel uncomfortable, but I'm sure you understand why we're all curious about you."

Sirena nodded and stared down into the depths of her cup. "I suppose all of you were at the chapel."

"Yes," Steve confirmed with a chuckle. "It was an interesting day, to say the least."

"It was the most mortifying day of my life," Sirena muttered, feeling more embarrassed then ever.

Steve chuckled again. "I can imagine, but if it makes you feel any better, I was silently cheering you on."

"Why?" Sirena asked, her embarrassment forgotten at his statement.

He gave an uneasy shrug, as if regretting his words. For a moment Sirena didn't think he'd answer, but then he said, "I liked Cynthia, but there was no depth to her. She reminded me of a pretty little doll that has to be wound up to walk and talk. I can understand her initial appeal to Noah, because she's the type of woman who radiates that helpless I-need-someone-to-take-care-of-me attitude that draws on a man's basic instincts. But her clinging-vine appeal would have quickly faded, because Noah needs a challenge. He'd have been bored within a month of their marriage."

Sirena arched a brow and said with a wry laugh, "If you believe that, I have this bridge I'd like to sell you."

Steve laughed heartily and his eyes were dancing when he responded with "If you can prove me wrong, I'll take you up on that proposition."

Sirena parted her lips to respond, only to hear Noah drawl, "If you value your job, Steve, you won't be taking my wife up on any proposition."

Sirena swung her head around and gaped at Noah in horror. The malevolent glare he had centered on his employee made her cringe.

Steve, however, seemed unperturbed by the threat or the look as he casually rose to his feet and grinned at his employer. "I value my job, Noah." He nodded toward Sirena then. "It was nice talking with you, Sirena."

"You, too," Sirena said. The moment Steve disappeared she leaped to her feet and turned on Noah. "You go out there right this minute and apologize to that man."

"Apologize?" Noah sneered as he stepped into the lounge and slammed the door behind him. "If anyone has any apologies to make around here, it's you. I may not be able to control your flirtatious bent at Barrington Foundation, but I can sure as hell control it here. This is my turf, Sirena, and don't you forget it."

"My flirtatious bent!" Sirena exclaimed furiously. "I don't have a flirtatious bone in my body, and even if I did, I was not flirting with Steve."

"It sure as hell sounded as if you were to me. I do have ears, Sirena, and they work perfectly."

"You also have the most irritating habit of taking everything you hear out of context. We were just being friendly."

"You were laughing with him, just like you were laughing with those two men yesterday when you were working on the furnace," he accused.

"You're jealous," she said in sudden and bemused understanding.

"Of course, I'm jealous," he snapped. "You never laugh with me. You only scream at me. How do you think it makes a man feel when every time he turns around his wife is having a good time with someone else."

"Did you ever stop to think that the reason I'm always screaming at you is because you're always yelling at me? Having a bellowing husband underfoot is not exactly a laughing matter, Noah."

"I don't bellow!" he bellowed.

Sirena merely grinned.

He continued to glare at her for a few moments, but then gave her a begrudging look. "Maybe I do bellow at times."

Sirena only arched a brow.

"All right," he muttered in disgust. "I bellow a lot, but it's only because you make me so . . ."

"Infuriated?" she offered.

He nodded.

"Frustrated?"

He nodded again.

"Annoyed?"

"You've made your point, Sirena."

"And you've made yours, Noah," she said as she walked to him. She reached out and straightened the collar of his knit pullover. Then she smiled up at him. "I kind of like the idea that you're jealous. It makes me feel special."

Noah stiffened. "Don't play games with me, Sirena."

"I'm not playing games," she replied honestly. "It does make me feel special. However, it would be a lot easier to handle if you didn't erupt like Mount Saint Helens every time I share a joke with a man. Somewhere along the line you have to grant me a little trust."

Noah relaxed as she continued to smile up at him. "It's not you I distrust, mermaid. It's your naïveté. You have absolutely no idea just how sexy you are. There are a lot of men who'd be happy to take advantage of that fact."

"Are you one of them?" she asked, feeling bold with the feminine power that surged through her at his words. It fascinated her to think that Noah—a man so gorgeous that three-quarters of the women she knew would give their eyeteeth to have him—would be jealous, and because he thought she was sexy, no less.

"Now you are playing games," he commented dryly. "In answer to your question, however, I have no intention of taking advantage of you."

Sirena's eyes flew wide open in surprise. "You don't?"

He shook his head and glanced down at his watch. "We'd better be on our way. We can make Gettysburg in time for lunch."

Sirena was so confused by his response that she didn't even object when he hurried her out of the building without giving her a chance to tell his employees goodbye.

Noah, on the other hand, wasn't feeling confused at all. In fact, he was feeling damn grim. The new computer program he'd just launched wasn't selling and he couldn't figure out why. He'd followed his marketing consultant's advice to the letter so he could hit his target market, but other than the initial flurry of questions from businesses who'd been intrigued with Ark II's unique features, interest seemed to have died completely. He'd been so sure of the program's success that he'd sunk nearly every penny of his business capital into the project. He had a million copies of the program sitting in his warehouse, and so far he'd only managed to sell 105 measly copies. He wasn't in danger of bankruptcy, but he was definitely in tight straits.

He supposed that was why he'd overreacted when he found Sirena and Steve laughing together in the lounge. He was sick and tired of hearing her laugh and joke with other people when he was doing well if he managed to get the time of day out of her.

Well, that wasn't exactly true, he amended. She had been more open with him since their little scene at the soup kitchen, but it still wasn't enough. The problem was, his patience was beginning to run out. He wasn't sure he'd be able to continue this friendship act much longer, particularly when he'd just given her the chance to flex her feminine muscle by confessing his jealousy. He'd seen the dawning realization of her power over him in her eyes, and he knew her well enough to understand that she'd eventually make an attempt to test that power. He had a feeling that when she did, he'd fold faster than a deck of cards.

Noah didn't know what frightened him more. The fact that Ark II could turn out to be a business disaster, or the possibility that Sirena could end up making him dance on the end of her strings.

SIRENA HAD NEVER BEEN to the Civil War battlegrounds at Gettysburg, and she quietly absorbed the history to which she was being exposed. Noah had first taken her on the auto tour that circled through the fields and hills where the battles had taken place. Afterward they went through the small museum at the visitors' center, and Sirena found the memorabilia disturbing. She was a pacifist at heart, although she was realistic enough to understand that man was a warrior by nature. She'd also basically agreed with the principles of national unity and freedom from slavery, but until now she'd never clearly understood what price had been paid for them. Her biggest shock as she followed Noah through the museum was just how ad-

vanced the weaponry had been, which explained why, at
the end of the three-day battle, there had been 51,000 cas-
ualties.

By the time they left the museum and walked across the
street to the Gettysburg National Cemetery she'd sunk into
a state of melancholy that only increased as they began to
pass the small white stones marking the graves of 3,700
Union soldiers killed in the battle. It was the graves of un-
identified soldiers that made her the saddest.

Noah, too, was feeling melancholy as he and Sirena
walked through the towering trees of the tranquil cemetery. When they reached the statue that commemorated
the site of President Lincoln's famous Gettysburg Address, he stopped beside Sirena and gazed out over the
semicircle of graves that surrounded them.

"What are you thinking?" he finally asked when she remained silent.

"I'm thinking of the rivers of tears that my fellow
women must have shed," she answered, a tiny crack in her
voice.

"I have a feeling that my fellow men shed just as many,"
Noah said softly as he wrapped an arm around her and
hugged her to his side. "They had to have believed in what
they were doing, mermaid. If they hadn't, the battle would
have never come to this. They would all have turned tail
and run."

"Oh, Noah," Sirena whispered as she turned in his arms
and rested her forehead against his shoulder.

Noah wrapped his arms around her and held her tight,
unable to stop the tears that dampened his eyes. He blinked
against the mist as he rested his chin against the top of her
head, wondering about the folly of men. War could be, he
knew, not only a matter of honor but a matter of necessity. What he couldn't understand was why the history

books and movies perpetually romanticized it. There was nothing romantic about the stark reality that lay in front of him.

"Let's leave here," Sirena said as she lifted her head and gazed up at him, looking forlorn.

He tenderly framed her face in his hands. "Of course, we'll leave. I didn't mean to upset you."

"You didn't upset me, Noah. The past did that all by itself. In fact, I'm glad you brought me here, and I'm glad that there are historic sites like this to visit."

Noah's expression was puzzled when he asked, "Why?"

"Because I take what I have for granted," she answered simply. *And because I also understand a more essential part of you,* she finished inwardly, and acknowledged that if she'd been in love with him before, she was now beyond redemption. Noah Samson was, she realized, a man worth fighting for, and Sirena had every intention of doing just that. She wanted to be Mrs. Noah Samson with every cell of her body. She also couldn't help but regret the two years she'd already thrown away. But if she had her way, she'd make up for every one of those lost days.

NOAH HAD HAD TO SPEND a day at his office. Ark II still wasn't moving, and he'd hoped to be able to come up with a battle plan by spending the day brainstorming with his staff. Unfortunately, it hadn't worked. They were as confused as he was by the fact that Ark II hadn't taken the industry by storm. It was revolutionary in design, which appeared to be its main problem. People were skeptical about whether it could live up to its claims.

His only solace was that Sirena had looked disappointed when he told her he had to go to Hagerstown to handle his business affairs. Their physical relationship still remained in limbo, but they were communicating better than ever. For the first time Noah was beginning to feel that a true reconciliation of their marriage was within reach.

"Good evening, Ben. How's life treating you?" Noah asked as he walked through the front door the servant had just opened for him.

"Fine, Mr. Samson," Ben stated, his lips twitching and his eyes twinkling as he eyed the huge bag of popcorn in Noah's hand. "And you, sir?"

"Never been better," Noah lied congenially. "And how about dropping the 'sir?' It makes me feel like an old coot. Can't you just call me Noah?"

"If you'd prefer me to do so, Mr. Noah."

"I'd prefer," Noah answered. "Is Sirena home?"

"She's in the sitting room with her mother and grandmother."

Noah arched a brow. "Is that good news or bad news?"

Ben gave a noncommittal shrug. "I believe you could interrupt."

"Which means it's bad news," Noah said with a sigh as he resolutely headed for the sitting room.

He'd quickly learned three things about life in the Barrington mansion. The first was that Ophelia Barrington ruled the roost. The second was that oil and water had a better chance of mixing than grandmother and granddaughter. The third was that Sirena's mother didn't know how to deal with either of them.

"I told you that it's none of your business," he heard Sirena state adamantly as he approached the sitting room.

"And I told you that as long as you live under my roof, it is my business," Ophelia stated just as adamantly.

"That can be easily rectified," Sirena said.

"Stop behaving like a child, Sirena," Ophelia scolded. "Every time you can't have your way you threaten to move out, and you know I'd never let you do that."

"Let me!" Sirena exclaimed loudly. "I'm twenty-six years old. You don't have the right to *let me* do anything."

"Sirena, would you please lower your voice," Pamela stated wearily.

"Why should I?" Sirena asked.

"Because there are people somewhere in the world who are trying to sleep," Noah said as he stepped through the doorway. "Good evening, Ophelia. Pamela."

"Thank heavens, you're home, Noah," Ophelia said. "Maybe you can talk some sense into this girl."

Noah glanced toward Sirena and winked. "Sirena is not a girl, Ophelia. She's a woman."

Ophelia made a noise that sounded suspiciously like an unladylike snort. "She's behaving like a child."

"Oh?" Noah drawled with a hint of teasing laughter in his voice. "What have you done now, Sirena?"

"I haven't done anything," she stated, glowering at her grandmother. "And I am not the one behaving like a child, *she* is."

Noah looked at Pamela. "I don't suppose you want to cast a deciding vote."

Pamela rolled her eyes heavenward. "I'm as neutral as Switzerland."

Noah nodded. "Smart move. Since I just walked in on this conversation, how about if someone fills me in on what's going on?"

Sirena and her grandmother started talking at the same time, their voices rising to deafening levels as they competed to be heard. Noah sighed and held up his hand for silence. When both women shut up, he looked at Pamela again.

"Pamela, what's going on?"

"Sirena wants Tabitha to go to work at the foundation."

"It's crazy," Ophelia said peevishly. "Tabitha has never worked a day in her life. She'd have a nervous breakdown before lunch."

"She would not," Sirena snapped. "She has a better grasp of business than I do."

"My point exactly," Ophelia snapped back. "I don't know why you insist on running that silly place, when you should be at home taking care of your husband."

"Silly place!" Sirena screeched.

"Time out!" Noah yelled.

When both women turned their glares on him, he calmly said, "Have either of you thought to ask Tabitha what she'd like to do?"

"No, they haven't," Tabitha announced as she walked through the door and came to a stop beside him. "But what else is new? The wallpaper around here gets treated with more respect than I do."

"That's not true!" Ophelia exclaimed.

"No, it's not true!" Sirena said just as ardently.

"Well, listen to that," Noah said with a grin. "Finally, the two of you agree on something."

"Even if they are both wrong," Tabitha muttered in disgust. "Well, I'm telling all of you right here and now that I'm tired of it. I'll soon be a half-century old, and I'm not going to be ordered around any longer. From this day forward, Tabitha Eleanor Barrington is an emancipated woman."

"Tabitha, what in the world has gotten into you?" Ophelia gasped as she threw her hand against her chest in a melodramatic gesture. "Do you want to put me in my grave?"

"No, Mother, I don't," Tabitha answered. "But if I don't start doing something, I'm going to be in my grave before you even have one foot in yours. I'm dying from boredom."

"But you're a gentlewoman!" Ophelia wailed.

"I'm fast becoming a dried-up old prune," Tabitha corrected impatiently.

"So, you will come to work for me!" Sirena stated in triumph.

"No," Tabitha replied as she switched her gaze to Sirena. "Barrington Foundation is your dream, Sirena, not mine. I'm going to work for Noah."

"What?" Sirena, Ophelia and Pamela exclaimed at the same time.

"Tabitha is going to work for me," Noah repeated as he dropped an arm around Tabitha's plump shoulders and gave them a fond squeeze. "I've been looking for a good sales representative in this area, and Tabitha fits my needs to a tee."

"But Tabitha doesn't know anything about computers," Ophelia stated.

"See, Noah?" Tabitha muttered as she looked up at him. "I've been going to college for four years, and no one even realized it. The lawn gets more attention around here than I do."

"That's not completely true," Noah corrected gently. "There is someone around here who knows exactly what you do."

"Yes," Tabitha agreed as she returned her gaze to her family. "Since I've already dropped one bombshell, I might as well drop the second. Ben and I are going steady."

Noah doubted that the Barrington household had ever been as silent as it was at Tabitha's announcement. He could have heard a pin drop.

"Ben?" Ophelia finally said. "*Our* Ben?"

"Yes, our Ben," Tabitha affirmed. "We've been dating for two years, and going steady for a year. If I have my way, we'll be engaged by Christmas."

"You're going to marry Ben?" Pamela questioned.

"If he asks me," Tabitha answered, her chin tilting up in a defiant gesture so reminiscent of Sirena that Noah automatically glanced toward his wife. She was staring at her aunt in openmouthed disbelief as Tabitha asked, "Do you have something to say about that, Pamela?"

Pamela smiled. "Just that I think it's wonderful."

"Me, too," Sirena echoed with a delighted laugh. "I can't think of a better couple."

"Mother?" Tabitha questioned as she switched her attention to her mother.

"Where in the world am I going to find someone to replace him?" Ophelia murmured.

"I don't want to be replaced," Ben stated as he joined the crowd.

"Well, of course, you do," Ophelia stated in disgruntlement. "You can't be my butler if you're my son-in-law."

"And why not?" he asked.

"Because . . . well, because who'll escort Tabitha when we have a party?"

"Mother, on the rare occasion that we have a party, we can always hire a temporary butler," Tabitha said in exasperation. "Besides, Ben hasn't asked me to marry him, so this discussion is moot."

"Well, he'd better ask you!" Ophelia stated as she glowered at a stone-faced Ben. "I still own a shotgun, Benjamin Hamilton."

"Mother!" Tabitha exclaimed in horror.

To everyone's surprise, Ben released a hearty belly laugh. Then he hugged Tabitha. "Let's make it official, Tabby. Will you marry me?"

"Of course," she said as she smiled up at him.

"Well, now that that's settled, we have a lot of work to do," Ophelia said as she rose to her feet. "Come along, Pamela, we have to plan a wedding."

When she reached Tabitha and Ben she stopped and regarded them for a long moment before smiling and reaching out to hug them both. "I couldn't be more pleased."

After they were all gone, Noah eyed Sirena cautiously as she turned and walked to the window that looked out over the rolling gardens surrounding the Barrington mansion. He tossed the bag of popcorn onto the small love seat and walked to her. Placing his hands on her shoulders, he drew her back against him, pleased when she allowed the action without complaint.

"How long have you known about Aunt Tabitha and Ben?" she asked.

"I figured it out a day or two after I'd been here."

"How come none of us saw what was going on?"

"Probably because you were too close to them."

"I didn't know she'd been going to school," Sirena said with a heartfelt sigh. "I saw her nose buried in books, but it's always been buried in books. I feel awful that I didn't even bother to look at the titles."

"Sirena, don't chide yourself. Her own mother didn't pay any attention to what she was doing."

"But you did," she said as she turned in his arms and peered up at him, her brow furrowed.

Noah stroked her frown lines. "Only by chance, mermaid."

"No, not by chance," Sirena stated in agitation. "You cared enough to look. We're all so damn callous, aren't we?"

"You're all very human," he told her. "I'd be as blind to my own family."

"I don't think so," Sirena said as she turned back to face the window. She tapped her fist against the windowsill in frustration. "I let her down. I should have been there for her, but I wasn't."

"If she'd wanted you there for her, she could have asked," he countered.

"But she shouldn't have had to ask!" Sirena exclaimed.

"Don't be ridiculous," Noah muttered as he forced her to turn back around and face him. "Why are you so upset about this? Aren't you happy for Tabitha and Ben?"

"Of course, I am."

"Then why do you look as if you're ready to chew on nails? Talk to me, Sirena. Tell me what's going on inside that delightful, but infuriating head of yours."

But Sirena couldn't tell him her thoughts, because he was the prime motivator of every one of them. If Noah had been so cognizant of what was happening between her aunt and the butler, he had to know that she was in love with him. Since he wouldn't acknowledge it, it meant he didn't return her feelings, and it made her feel so sad inside that she wanted to sit down and cry.

"What's the popcorn for?" she asked as she transferred her gaze to the large bag he'd tossed onto the love seat, deciding that it was time she distracted them both from a conversation that was destined for disaster.

Noah knew she was changing the subject, and he resisted the urge to shake her when she refused to talk to him.

"*The African Queen* is on television tonight. I know it's your favorite movie, and I thought we'd watch it together."

"And you bought popcorn? Mrs. Mullen could have fixed us some popcorn, Noah. We have advanced that far in the Barrington mansion."

"But this is theater popcorn," he said. "I even had them put on extra butter."

"You remembered," she said softly as she crossed to the love seat and lifted the bag, resisting the urge to hug it to her chest. "I love extra butter."

"I know." When she looked at him with melting eyes, he glanced at his watch. It was the only way he could maintain control. "In my room in fifteen minutes. Dress is casual, and don't forget the popcorn. And Sirena?"

"Yes?"

"Bring your own tissues. My supply is running low."

WHEN AN ADVERTISEMENT came on, Sirena sniffed and dabbed at her eyes with a tissue from the box she'd brought with her. Then she burrowed her hand into the bag of popcorn that sat between her and Noah on his bed as she said, "It's so romantic, isn't it?"

"Actually, I think Bogart's henpecked," Noah replied around a mouthful of popcorn.

"Noah!" she chided. "He can't be henpecked. They aren't married."

Noah grinned at her. "A mere technicality."

"How can you make fun of such a romantic, not to mention classic, movie?" she asked with mild irritation.

"I'm not making fun of it. I'm just putting it into perspective. Come on, mermaid, do you really think that you and I could go through all of that together and not tear each other's throats out?"

"We're talking about fantasy, not reality."

"And is that what you want?" he asked as he gazed at her thoughtfully. "Do you want fantasy, mermaid?"

"Sometimes," she answered.

"Why?"

She shrugged. "There are days when I find reality too harsh, especially at the foundation. No matter how much I do, it's never enough."

Noah wrapped his arm around her shoulder and snuggled her against his side. "You do more than your share, Sirena, and no single man or woman can cure the ills of the world."

"I know, but there's still a part of me that wants to do exactly that. Pretty silly, huh?"

"I don't think it's silly at all," Noah replied as he gazed down into her upturned face. "I think the sentiment is as beautiful as you are."

"I'm not beautiful, Noah," she said, "and I think we've had this conversation before."

"We have," he agreed. "And you are beautiful, Sirena. Take my word for it."

Sirena reached up and smoothed her fingers over the lock of hair that had tumbled across his forehead. "You're a very sweet man, Noah Samson."

Noah arched a brow at that line. "I'll remind you of that the next time you're yelling at me."

"Do you know that we haven't yelled at each other once during this past week?" she asked.

"Yes," he answered smugly. "I told you we could get along."

"Maybe it's just the calm before the storm. We're both too hotheaded for it to last forever."

"Good heavens, Sirena. Even the most tranquil people in the world lose their tempers on occasion."

"My mother doesn't," Sirena mused. "She scolds every now and then, but I've never actually seen her angry. I suppose it had to do with her background."

"And what's her background?" Noah inquired, curious about Pamela, who still remained an enigma.

"Her parents were child abusers," Sirena told him. "By the time she was ten years old, they'd broken nearly every bone in her body at one time or another."

"How could that happen and the law not step in?" Noah asked in horrified disbelief.

"Because in those days no one considered child abuse a crime," Sirena answered. "Her parents were also extremely wealthy and wielded more power than the Barringtons have ever had, so who was going to go after them? My mother once told me that if they hadn't been killed she was sure they would have eventually beaten her to death."

"How did they die?" Noah asked next.

"In a hotel fire while vacationing in France. She came to Harrisburg to live with her aunt and uncle, who doted upon her. That's when she met my father. She was ten and he was twelve, and she said she thought he was the most obnoxious, irritating boy she'd ever met in her life."

Noah tangled his fingers in her hair, fascinated by the way it clung to his fingers. "Perhaps he was only being obnoxious and irritating because he was afraid of the feelings he had for her."

Sirena gave him a considering look. "You're the most obnoxious and irritating man I know, Noah. Are you that way because you're afraid of your feelings for me?" she asked bravely.

Noah caught his breath at the question, and as he continued to stare down at her, he knew that his answer had to be a resounding yes. Sirena drew on every facet of his personality. She brought out the best and the worst in him. He knew in that moment that he was also head over heels, heart on his sleeve in love with her.

"I think," he stated quietly but firmly, "that it's time you went back to your own room."

"And if I refuse?"

"Then you'll have to deal with the consequences. Are you ready to do that, Sirena? Are you ready to commit yourself?"

"I'm not sure what I'd be committing myself to," she answered.

"In that case, I know it's time for you to go," he said as he levered himself off the bed. "You can take the rest of the popcorn with you."

"Noah, I think we should talk about this," she said as she stared at his stiff back.

Noah shook his head. "Another time, Sirena."

"But . . ."

"Dammit, Sirena, get out of here before I do something we'll both regret!" he all but roared as he spun around to face her.

Sirena's entire nervous system went on red alert at the sensual threat. Her body begged her to stay, but her mind argued for self-preservation. Her mind won as she met his stormy eyes. She scrambled off the bed and hurried through the connecting bath into her room, leaving the popcorn behind.

When she'd locked the door behind her, she leaned against it and drew in a deep breath. She wasn't ready to commit herself, she insisted firmly. They still had such a long way to go before they could even begin to build. They had to have time to get to know each other. They had to prove that they could get along. She had to be reassured that Noah could accept who and what she was. That he could be secure enough in their relationship to introduce her to his family.

But hours later she was still tossing and turning in her bed, unable to curb the yearning that clawed at her insides. If she'd stayed with Noah tonight he would have

made love to her, and she wanted him to make love to her.
However, she couldn't indulge herself in physical pleasure just to soothe her libido. He'd asked her if she was
ready for a commitment, but he hadn't offered his own
commitment in return.

Another hour passed before she hit the light on her
alarm clock and noted the lateness of the hour. What she
needed was a breath of fresh air, she decided. She rose
from bed and walked toward the sliding glass doors and
the balcony she rarely used, surprised to find the door unlocked.

She slid it back and stepped onto the balcony, drawing
in a deep breath and then another. She'd been standing
there for several minutes before she saw Noah standing at
the other end, his elbows braced on the railing as he stared
up at the night sky.

"Noah, is something wrong?" she asked, walking toward him. Startled he spun toward her and Sirena's heart
wrenched at the torment in his eyes. "Noah, what is it?"

He held up his hand to stop her progress toward him,
gruffly saying, "Sirena, just go back to bed."

"Not until you tell me what's wrong," she said as she
took another step toward him.

But he didn't need to answer. The heat in his eyes said
it all as they poured down her gossamer nightgown, and
Sirena's knees began to shake as suppressed desire began
to flow through her.

"Make love to me," she said hoarsely.

Noah's head shot up and he searched her face, seeing the
confusion in her eyes. He knew that all he had to do was
step forward and pull her into his arms and she'd be his.
But he didn't want one night of sexual gratification, he
wanted all of her, forever.

"Be sure of your invitation, Sirena," he told her. "If I make love to you I'll consider it a reconciliation of our marriage and I'll never grant you a divorce. You'll be my wife forever."

Sirena shivered at the ominous presentiment his words evoked. Was she willing to take such a large step? She wanted him and she loved him, but none of her doubts had been appeased. He was making her no promises, giving her no concessions.

She stared at him, willing him to offer her something that she could latch on to. But he was regarding her through eyes shielded by a screen of long black lashes that hid his thoughts from her.

She'd be crazy to go to him, she thought. But then she heard her mother's words echoing in her ears: *"Fear is a powerful motivator, Sirena. It's also our best weapon if we want to defeat ourselves."*

"I'm not going to let fear defeat me," Sirena stated as she walked toward him.

"What?" Noah said in confusion.

"Nothing," Sirena said as she reached him and wrapped her arms around his neck. "Kiss me, Noah. Then make love to me."

Noah peered down at her warily. "I meant what I said, Sirena. If I make love to you, you'll be my wife forever."

"That works both ways, Noah Samson, and heaven help you if you so much as look at another woman."

The feelings rushing through him were so intense that Noah had to consciously relax his hold on Sirena. Otherwise, he was certain he would crack one or two of her ribs.

"I don't think that will be a problem," he murmured as he lowered his lips to hers. "In fact," he sighed as he released her lips and lifted her into his arms, "I don't think I'll have time to look at another woman."

"Believe me, you won't," Sirena said with conviction as she wrapped her arms around his neck and treated him to a kiss so potent that Noah barely made it back to his bed.

10

"I SWORE this time was going to be gentle," Noah rasped as he dropped Sirena onto his bed and came over her.

Sirena arched her hips to meet his, trembling as she met his straining denim-clad loins. "Why should it be different this time?" she asked in a sultry voice, memories from the past engulfing her.

He tangled his fingers in her hair as he peered down into her face with solemn concern. "Because this is a new beginning, mermaid. I want it to be unforgettable."

Sirena smiled as she stroked his hair off his forehead and touched the hard planes of his cheekbones. She caressed the small scar on his left cheek, traced the uneven line of his broken nose.

"With you, it's always been unforgettable," she said huskily.

"Oh, Sirena." He sighed as he caught her lips in a kiss that stole the breath from her lungs and the strength from her limbs.

Sirena could only cling to him as his hands explored her with a tender grace that tantalized and teased, making her ache to the very marrow of her bones.

He stripped her nightgown over her head and his lips skimmed down her throat to her chest, tormenting one nipple and then the other of her upthrust breasts.

"Noah!" she gasped as his lips moved lower, exploring her concave abdomen.

"It's okay," he reassured her as her fingers dug into his shoulders. His breath stirred the golden red curls that protected her femininity. "Relax, mermaid. Just relax and let me love you."

Relaxation was the last thing on Sirena's mind as his mouth and tongue honored her in a way she'd never experienced before, and she felt helpless as he brought her to the brink of desire and left her hovering.

"Let it go!" he rasped when he felt her struggling against his intimate kisses. "Let me love you, Sirena."

She continued to fight against the wave of pleasure that threatened to succumb her, but then it became so powerful that she was no longer in control. It washed over her in warm, satisfying waves that curled her toes and tightened her thighs around him.

Noah was smiling in satisfaction as he levered himself over her, his clothes miraculously gone. "Now it's my turn," he whispered throatily as he thrust into her.

Sirena gasped at his entrance and he immediately stilled. He seemed to sense when her body had accustomed itself to his fit, and he began to move in a slow, tantalizing dance that had her once again hovering on the brink.

She couldn't touch enough of him. Her hands flew over his lean ribs, his muscled back, his taut buttocks and his bulging thighs. All the while, her lips roamed over his face, his neck, his chest, homing in on his nipples, which peeked out from enticing whorls of dark hair.

His groans of pleasure urged her on. His urgent rhythm sent her to soaring heights. His body demanded, and she responded on cue until they were flying, clinging to each other in heady ecstasy as they reached a shattering climax that left them gasping for breath.

"It's never been better," Noah murmured in her ear as he collapsed against her and rolled so that she was cradled against his chest. He buried his hands in her hair and flexed his fingers against her scalp.

"It's never been better," she agreed in satisfaction as she curled around him, reluctant to break the intimate joining they still shared.

One of his hands continued to massage her scalp, while the other began to move down her body, kneading and stroking her muscles.

Long minutes passed before he said, "Sirena?"

"Mmm-hmm?" she hummed lazily.

He rubbed his hand against the back of her thigh. "I was in such a hurry to make love to you that I didn't think about . . ."

Sirena arched her head back so she could see his face, instinctively knowing his concern. "It's all right, Noah. I'm protected."

She blinked when he scowled at her and asked tersely, "You're on the pill?"

"No. I just have faith in the rhythm method."

"You what?" he roared as he sat bolt upright in bed, sending her sprawling across the mattress. "You've been practicing the rhythm method for two years? Are you crazy?"

"No," she said complacently as she curled into a fetal ball, smiled at him and pulled the cover up to her chin.

"No, what?" he demanded with enough vehemence to make another woman cower.

"No, I haven't been practicing the rhythm method for two years, and no, I'm not crazy," she said with a grin.

"Sirena, you have exactly five seconds to explain that statement," Noah stated as he leaned over her and braced a hand on either side of her head.

"Birth control hasn't been a problem, Noah, because I haven't gone to bed with anyone else."

To say Noah looked shocked would have been like saying that money wasn't green.

"What about the old coot?" he pressed.

"Our relationship hadn't progressed that far."

Noah's grin was almost wolfish with delight.

"Stop looking so self-satisfied," Sirena grumbled as she reached up, circled her arms around his neck and pulled him down to her pillow. "In another month or two I might have gone to bed with Jonathan."

His eyes were so close that Sirena had to lean her head backward to keep from crossing her own. "What?" she asked disgruntledly when he continued to grin at her.

He slid his hand down her body, caught the back of her knee and levered her leg over his. "I'm it?"

His manhood was stirring against her, and she asked suggestively, "Are we playing hide-and-seek?"

"You're damn right," he growled. "I'm going to seek, and you're going to hide me."

And they made love again. But this time it was slow, leisurely and physically draining. Sirena was instantly asleep when Noah shifted her head onto his arm.

But even though Noah's body demanded that he join her in her slumber, he couldn't help but wallow in pleasure at her revelation. He was her first and only lover and he was determined to be her last. He'd just feel better if he knew that his business was on better footing. It was still a struggle for him to accept Sirena's wealth, particularly when combined with the fact that she was quite successful in her business endeavors while Noah's Ark was floundering.

But as Noah's pride tried to surface, he held it back. For once in his life, he was going to concentrate on what was important, and Sirena was more important than his damnable Samson pride. He loved her, and tonight she'd committed herself to their marriage. He'd endure a stake through his heart before he walked away from that commitment.

With a loving smile, he pressed a kiss against her forehead before snuggling up against her. She was his again and no one and nothing would ever make him let her go. They were bound together for better or for worse. He'd just feel better if they weren't starting out with the worst.

SIRENA MURMURED in protest when a pair of lips nibbled at her neck and then her ear.

"Wake up, mermaid," Noah whispered. "Mrs. Mullen will arrive with breakfast in just a few minutes, and I want you awake enough to enjoy it."

Sirena's eyes flew open at his words and she jerked her head toward him. "Mrs. Mullen is on her way up?"

He nodded.

"Oh, no!" Sirena exclaimed as she began to scramble out of bed. "I have to get back to my room."

She let out a small "oomph" when Noah grabbed her around the waist and hauled her back into bed.

"Just where do you think you're going?" he asked as he braced himself over her.

"Noah, if I don't get out of here, Mrs. Mullen will know exactly what we've been doing!"

"So?" he asked, his scowl deepening. "You are my wife, Sirena, and Mrs. Mullen doesn't have that title in front of her name because she's spent her life in a convent."

"But don't you understand?" Sirena wailed. "By the time she gets downstairs everyone is going to know what we've done."

"And what exactly have we done?" he asked ominously.

Sirena blushed. "I knew you could be callous, Noah, but I always thought you had a fairly good memory."

"My memory is perfect. What I'm having difficulty understanding is why my wife doesn't want the household to know that she's been performing her wifely duties."

"Wifely duties?" she all but screeched. "You arrogant son of a—"

Noah kissed her, and it wasn't a gentle kiss but one meant to cow with passion. It worked perfectly. She was clinging to him when he pulled away.

"A son of a what?" he questioned with a superior grin.

"Blacksmith," she grumbled. "You don't play fair, Noah."

"Honey, this isn't play," he drawled as he slid his hand beneath the covers and touched her until she was straining against his hand. "Still want to run and hide and play innocent?"

Sirena groaned and tossed her arm over her eyes. "This is so embarrassing, Noah. What is everyone going to think?"

"Well, since both your grandmother and your mother had three children, and Ben and Tabitha are having their own close encounter of the intimate kind, I assume that they'll all understand." Noah began to ease the covers down with a wolfish grin.

"Stop it," Sirena ordered as she fought him over the covers. "Mrs. Mullen is on her way up with breakfast, remember?"

"I'll put a Do Not Disturb sign on the door."

"Over my dead body!"

"That wouldn't be any fun," he said with a chuckle as he hauled her beneath him.

"You're testing my patience, Noah," Sirena warned.

"That's not all I want to test, mermaid," he murmured as he kissed her again.

He reluctantly let her come up for air at the knock on the door, and he slid out of bed and into his denims in one smooth motion.

Sirena ducked under the covers, deciding that even death wouldn't rescue her from this humiliation. She wanted to groan again as she listened to Noah and Mrs. Mullen exchange pleasantries and plan Sirena's and Noah's meals for the entire weekend. To listen to the man, you'd think he was out for a stroll in the park, she grumbled inwardly. The worst part was, it was Saturday morning, so she couldn't even claim work as a reason to crawl out of bed. Her timing for capitulation had definitely been off.

"Heads up," Noah stated cheerfully as she felt his weight settle on the mattress. "We have enough calories here to get us to lunchtime, and Mrs. Mullen promises to feed us through the remainder of the weekend."

Sirena peeped out from beneath the covers. "I am not a sex object, Noah Samson."

He reached out and tweaked the end of her nose. "No, you're not. You're a grumpy morning person, so I'll indulge you."

"You're infuriating."

He nodded his agreement and offered her a bite of toast. Sirena took it grudgingly and chewed ominously while she watched him smother the rest of the piece of toast in honey. When he sighed in satisfaction as he bit into the bread, Sirena experienced a need for revenge. She also knew precisely how to exact it.

She sat up, the covers once again clenched to her chest, but she let them droop as she leaned toward him and examined the food on the tray straddled over his lap. Noah's intake of breath encouraged her and she let the covers drop an inch lower.

"I'm absolutely starving," she said in a sultry drawl. Then she raised rounded eyes to his face. "Are you going to hog the tray?"

His eyes were glued to her breasts and the covers that barely hid her nipples. "Help yourself, Sirena."

"Why, thank you, Noah," she crooned. She let the covers drop to her waist, lifted a piece of toast and the spoon from the honey jar, which dripped onto his flat stomach. When he sucked in another breath, she raised innocent eyes to his face. "How clumsy of me. Let me clean you up."

Before he could object, she lowered her head and licked the honey from his skin, letting her tongue move closer and closer to his belly button.

"Mermaid, you're asking for trouble," he growled as she slipped her tongue into the small indentation.

She shivered in anticipation of his sensual threat. "Get out of those jeans and I'll give you a good example of just how much trouble I can get into. In fact, I think we could deplete our supply of honey. You are a very big man, Noah," she murmured suggestively.

His groan should have been enough to satisfy her revenge, but it wasn't. Sirena wanted to give him the same pleasure he'd given her last night. She slid her hand beneath the tray and seductively touched the swell of his manhood, reveling in her power when he jerked spasmodically beneath her hand.

"Well, Noah?" she inquired as she glanced up at him.

"I think," he stated tautly, "that I'm a goner."

With that, he thrust the honey pot into her hands, dropped the tray to the side of the bed and lifted his hips to dispose of his jeans.

When he lay before her naked and vulnerable, he met her eyes. "Be gentle with me, mermaid," he stated hoarsely. "I'm simply a mortal man."

"Gentle is my middle name," she said, very hoarse herself, as she lifted the spoon and began to dribble honey over him. "And although I'll agree that you're a mortal man, there isn't anything simple about you."

Noah's answer was a harsh but endearing curse as she lowered her head.

A WEEKEND IN BED with Noah was almost worth facing the knowing looks of the Barrington matrons when Sirena arrived downstairs for breakfast early Monday morning. Almost, but not quite. She tried to hide her blush as she sat down at the breakfast table and reached for the platter of scrambled eggs.

"Where's Noah?" her grandmother asked with suspicious innocence.

"In the shower," Sirena answered as she dropped a spoonful of eggs onto her plate and reached for the platter of ham.

"It was considerate of him to let you go first," Pamela murmured, and Sirena almost dropped her slice of ham on the Irish linen tablecloth.

Noah hadn't let her go first. In fact, they'd shared the shower and Sirena had discovered the rewards of conserving water.

"Noah can be a considerate man when he wants to be," Sirena muttered.

She choked on her orange juice when Tabitha said, "Good heavens, why are we all dancing around the maypole? It's wonderful that you and Noah have finally resolved your differences, Sirena. When do you think you'll be ready to start a family?"

"Aunt Tabitha!" Sirena exclaimed in a scolding voice. "What in the world has gotten into you?"

"I'd say it's love," Ophelia stated as she smiled at Tabitha indulgently, before shifting less indulgent eyes toward Sirena. "She's right, you know. You are twenty-six, Sirena, and Noah's nearly thirty-two."

"Well, remind me to run right down to Social Security and register for our pensions," Sirena huffed.

Pamela chuckled before saying, "Leave the child alone. She and Noah have plenty of time."

"Plenty of time for what?" asked Noah, exercising his knack for arriving at the most inauspicious moment.

"To give me great-grandchildren," Ophelia answered. "You'd better hurry up, Noah. I'm getting older every day."

"You're timeless, Ophelia," Noah stated gallantly as he sat down beside Sirena and slipped his hand beneath the table, giving her knee a reassuring squeeze. "Besides, I understand that you already have five great-grandchildren. Sirena and I wouldn't want to steal their thunder."

"But they live thousands of miles away," Ophelia answered sullenly. "I want a great-grandchild close at hand that I can spoil until it's so rotten it stinks."

"A wonderful incentive to run right out and get pregnant," Sirena grumbled. "Maybe that's why Stefan and Damon decided to move to California."

"Sirena, that was uncalled for," her mother immediately chastised.

Sirena raised her head to retaliate, but the words died on her lips as she met her mother's hurt eyes. Suddenly, realization hit her.

"They did move so far away to get away from the three of you, didn't they?"

Her mother, aunt and grandmother exchanged covert looks. Finally Pamela said, "They wanted to find their own identity."

"In other words, you let them go without a whimper, but you've refused to even let me move out of the house!"

"Sirena, calm down," Noah stated quietly.

"Calm down?" she repeated as she swung her head toward him, her eyes filled with tears. "I've accused you of chauvinism, but you don't even hold a candle to these three! For years they've been dumping guilt on my head, and it's only because I'm the last of the Barrington guilt club. Nothing I do is good enough for them. They don't have any pride in me or my accomplishments. All they care about is that they maintain control over the last chick in the nest, because the other two told them where to get off."

"Sirena, that's not true," her mother stated plaintively. "We are proud of you, and we've never meant to make you feel guilty. But you aren't like your brothers. You're so . . . impetuous."

"Yes," her grandmother agreed. "Look at your past record, Sirena. You got kicked out of one private school after another. When you finally made it to college, you skipped from one college to another. You'd no more than gotten your degree than you eloped with Noah after knowing him for less than two days. Three weeks later you arrive on the doorstep with the announcement that you'd just gotten a Mexican divorce. Then, when you discovered that your divorce wasn't legal, it was Noah who told us. You didn't even have the courtesy to give us that news!"

"Mother, you're being too severe," Tabitha stated bravely.

"Severe?" Ophelia echoed shrilly. "She's a child!"

"I am not a child!" Sirena yelled. "I am a full-grown woman, and if I haven't measured up to your expectations, then it's your fault. The three of you did this to me."

"Sirena, calm down," Noah stated again.

"I am not going to clam down!" she railed at him. "They make me sound as if I'm incompetent, but they don't tell you that I got kicked out of private school after private school because they pulled me out of public school, took me away from all my friends and stuck me into a world in which I didn't belong. I hated being driven to school every morning and picked up every afternoon by the chauffeur. My brothers weren't forced into that world, Noah. They got on the school bus every day and went to public school with the friends they'd had since kindergarten."

"When your brothers went to school your father was alive," Pamela stated urgently. "After he died, it was just the three of us. We wanted to protect you."

"By taking me away from everything I knew? Everyone I loved?" Sirena questioned as angry tears sprang to her eyes. She dashed at them impatiently, rose to her feet and threw her napkin on the table. "I'll be moved out by nightfall."

"Sirena, you don't mean that!" her mother exclaimed as she leaped to her feet and reached across the table as if to get a firm grasp on her daughter.

Sirena backed up several steps, shaking her head. "I mean it, Mother, and for once in your life, don't try to stop me. I don't belong here. I've never belonged here. I'm not one of you. I'm me."

With that, she spun on her heel and ran from the room.

When Pamela rounded the table to go after her, Noah rose to his feet and caught her arm. "Let me handle this, Pamela."

"But, Noah, you don't understand. She's got it all wrong. Everything I did, I did to protect her," Pamela said on a sob.

"I know," Noah said as he pulled her into his arms and gave her a hug. "But you also have to see Sirena's side.

She's not a little girl, Pamela, and she hasn't been one for a long time. She grew up and you didn't see it."

"Ha!" Ophelia exclaimed in disgust. "She's just a child."

Noah swung his head toward the older woman and leveled an admonishing gaze on her. "Sirena is not a child, Ophelia. However, you are a tyrant."

"How dare you?" Ophelia stated haughtily as she stiffened regally in her chair.

"I dare, because it's the truth," Noah answered. "Leave my wife alone, Ophelia. If you don't, you're going to answer to me."

Ophelia opened her mouth to respond, but Tabitha blithely interrupted with, "It's true, Mother. You are a tyrant." When Ophelia turned a murderous glare on her daughter, Tabitha simply smiled and said, "If you're foolish enough to tangle with Noah, you'd better be redefining your definition of childish, because you'll surely fall into that category."

"Tabitha!" Ophelia muttered in horror. "What *has* gotten into you?"

"Call it adolescent rebellion about forty years too late," Tabitha answered as she lifted her orange juice glass in a mock toast. "Believe it or not, Mother, the world does not revolve around you."

"Why I never!" Ophelia exclaimed.

"No, you never did," Pamela agreed as she pushed herself away from Noah. "The worst part of this entire situation is that I let you bully me into doing what you thought was right, because I didn't know how to survive without Alex. You drove my sons off and now you're driving my daughter away. Well, Ophelia, I'm not going to stand by and let you do it this time, do you hear me?"

Noah decided it was time for him to go check on Sirena, and he eased himself out of the room as the three women moved on to the next stage of battle.

Ben stood in the hallway, and he gave Noah a resigned smile as he rolled his eyes toward the ceiling.

"You're a saint, Ben," Noah muttered. "If you need the cavalry, let me know."

"I've handled the three of them for years," the older man stated calmly. "I'm sure I can handle them now. You just take care of Sirena."

Noah nodded as he headed up the stairs. He knocked on Sirena's door, and when she didn't answer, he entered uninvited.

She glared at him over her shoulder, muttered what sounded suspiciously like a curse and walked back to her closet. She began to toss garment after garment into the suitcase on her bed until it was overflowing. When she returned to the closet, Noah began to unpack her bag.

"Noah Samson, just what do you think you're doing?" she demanded when she turned from the closet and he passed her to hang up his armload of clothes.

"You're not going to run away from them, Sirena," he said as he placed the clothes on the rack and turned back to rescue the ones from her arms. "You're going to fight it out to the bloody end."

"You are not my boss, and I'll do exactly what I want to do," she stated mutinously.

"Fine," he said, stepping back from the closet and opening his arms wide, letting her clothes drop to the floor. "Tuck your tail between your legs and run, Sirena. Just realize that when you do, you've given credence to every one of your grandmother's claims. You've lowered yourself to the child that she's claiming you are."

"I am not a child, and I'm perfectly capable of taking care of myself."

"Of course, you are," he agreed easily. "You know that, and I know that, but you haven't proved it to anyone else in this house. When they push, you fold, because it's easier to run than to fight. Stop running and face them head-on. You're strong enough to do it. My word, you run a business that would make my head spin. But you do it, Sirena, and you do it well. If you want them to acknowledge your accomplishments, then you have to hold up your head. You have to show that you've risen above them, and you've done it in spite of them. Don't become another Tabitha. Don't wait until you're fifty years old before you find the guts to take that stand."

Sirena collapsed on the foot of the bed and buried her face in her hands. She desperately wanted to cry, but the tears simply wouldn't come.

"You don't understand, Noah. You just don't understand."

"Yes, I do," he stated as he sat down beside her and held her close. "All your life you've been in a push-pull situation, but it isn't unique to you, Sirena. I've had the same problem with my family. I'm the first one who's said to hell with farming and gone out to get a college degree. I'm the first one to open my own business. I've broken the mold, and a part of them cheers me on for it, while another part of them is frightened by it. Put yourself in your family's place. It's scary for them to see someone they love doing something that they don't understand. It's your obligation to make them understand what you're doing and why you're doing it."

"I don't know if I'm strong enough," she whispered as she raised dry, feverish eyes to his face. "They're so strong."

Noah caught her hands in his and peered down into her face, willing her to latch on to his own strength. "You're stronger, Sirena. Look at what you've built, and you've done it all by yourself. You can fight them and you can win. You've already done that with Barrington Foundation. Now it's time to do it for yourself."

When she still looked torn, he said, "Have I told you how proud I am of you?"

She shook her head. "Why would you be proud of me?"

"Because I did my best to tear you down two years ago. I was worse than the matrons. At least they had family protection on their side. All I had was my own fears and insecurities. I said terrible things to you, and I regret every one of them."

"I deserved everything you said. I was shallow and selfish and spoiled and—"

"—loving and giving and kind and gentle," he finished with vehemence. "I picked up where the matrons left off, and I did it because I was running scared. I was madly in love with you, and I didn't think I deserved you. I had to make you less than me so I could think more of myself."

"You loved me?" she whispered, her brain having halted at those three words.

"I did and I do," Noah stated as he pulled her against him and hugged her so tightly his arms ached. "I love you, mermaid, and I always will."

"Oh, Noah." The words came as a half sob and as she clung to him her pent-up tears began to fall. Barringtons don't cry, she reminded herself, though all she'd seemed to do since Noah burst back into her life was cry. But she didn't feel shamed by her tears, because they felt healing and honest. "I love you, too. I always have and I always will."

"Well, you don't have to cry about it," he murmured as he caught her chin and tilted her head upward, brushing away her tears. "It shouldn't be that painful."

"It's not. It's just that . . ."

"It's just that what?" he asked gently as he pushed the damp tendrils away from her face.

"I don't deserve you."

"Boy, if that isn't the pot calling the kettle black," he said in teasing chastisement. "I think, Sirena, that we deserve each other."

"For better or for worse," she said on a hiccup.

"For richer or for poorer," he whispered as he drew her forward for a kiss. "Let's finish unpacking you later."

"Yes, much later," Sirena agreed as she pushed him down to her bed.

"Aren't you due at the foundation pretty soon?" he asked as she straddled him and began to pull off his tie.

"I think I have a few hours of comp time coming."

He grinned up at her when her hands moved to the buttons on his shirt. "But what about me? I'm only a lowly consultant."

"You are low," she stated with a teasing laugh as she dropped down onto his chest, "but give me ten minutes, and I'll have you higher than you've ever dreamed."

Noah chuckled as he rolled and pulled her beneath him. "I always have been a firm believer in upward mobility."

"I can confirm the upward," she taunted as she unzipped his slacks. "The mobility part you'll have to prove to me."

"What are consultants for, if not to prove a point?" Noah said with a laugh as he began to peel off her dress.

"I do love you, Noah," she whispered as his hand slid into her bodice.

"And I love you. Just remember, mermaid, that together we stand. Divided we fall."

"I've already forgotten my division tables," Sirena mumbled as he relieved her of her bra.

"You always were a considerate woman," he murmured as he caught one pert nipple between his lips.

Sirena had a million quick comebacks to that line, but she couldn't think of one of them. All she knew was that the man she loved also loved her. The matrons no longer mattered. The past no longer mattered. She was going to indulge herself in the present and let tomorrow worry about itself.

11

SIRENA AND NOAH were sitting in her office discussing the best way to computerize some of her files when her receptionist buzzed and announced that the Barrington matrons were here to see her. Sirena shot a nervous glance toward Noah, who gave her a reassuring smile, and she told the receptionist to send them in.

Seconds later, the door opened and Ophelia swept into the room, with Pamela and Tabitha trailing behind her. Ophelia glanced around the room and frowned.

"Good heavens, Sirena, you need to hire a decorator. This place looks like a used furniture store."

Sirena automatically bristled at the comment. "I have more important things to spend my money on than furniture, Grandmother. You know, things like food and clothes and shelter for the needy and the homeless."

Ophelia seemed to consider Sirena's statement and then nodded, after which she promptly sat down in a chair in front of Sirena's desk, gesturing for Pamela to take the one beside her.

"Tabitha, take my seat," Noah offered as he rose and went to stand behind Sirena, casually dropping his hands on her shoulders.

He could feel the tension in her muscles and he lightly massaged them. He'd expected another confrontation between the four women, but he hadn't expected the matrons to come to Sirena's office for the showdown. He smiled to himself when Ophelia stared at Sirena, waiting for her to open the conversation, and Sirena merely stared back in mute rebellion. He was also pleased to note that the thicker the tension became between them, the more Sirena relaxed beneath his hands. She was ready for battle, and he had a feeling that she would win this round.

Finally, it was Tabitha who broke the silence by saying, "Good heavens, Mother, would you stop trying to save face and say what you've come to say?"

Ophelia shot a quelling look at Tabitha and grumbled something inarticulate before returning her gaze to Sirena.

"We've come to apologize, Sirena."

Sirena leaned back in her chair and said, "Okay."

Ophelia's lips lifted in a wry smile. "You're going to make me say the words, aren't you?"

Sirena nodded.

Her grandmother released a resigned sigh. "All right, I'm sorry for treating you like a child. I'm sorry for not giving you credit for what you've done here. I'm sorry for trying to control your life."

Pamela picked up where Ophelia left of by saying, "I'm sorry for not fighting harder for your rights. I'm sorry for letting Ophelia run roughshod over both of us instead of us standing behind you."

It was Tabitha's turn and she smiled as she said, "I'm sorry for being such a woebegone wimp that I didn't step in and defend you against both of them."

Sirena eyed the three for a long moment, before responding with, "And I apologize to all three of you. I should have sat down and talked to you, instead of getting into a shouting match every time my feelings were hurt, or I felt I was being treated wrongly. If I wanted to be treated as an adult, then I should have behaved like one."

"So you won't move out," Pamela said in relief.

Sirena shook her head. "Noah and I will be moving."

"But why?" Ophelia asked in sincere distress. "There's plenty of room for you at the mansion."

"I realize that," Sirena said. "However, Noah's business is in Hagerstown, and I think we should find a place somewhere in between so we can split the mileage difference."

"But that means you'll be commuting," Ophelia objected. "Sirena, driving a long distance like that every day increases your chances for an accident. Use your head for once and—"

"Ophelia, drop it," Pamela muttered. "This is none of our business."

"Pamela's right, Mother," Tabitha said. "Put a button on it."

"Well!" Ophelia exclaimed with a huff and crossed her arms over her chest.

Sirena glanced up at Noah, and he winked at her. She returned her gaze to the matrons and asked, "Was there anything else?"

Pamela caught her bottom lip between her teeth and worried at it.

"Mother?" Sirena finally prodded.

Pamela drew in a deep breath and said, "Since Tabitha and Ben are getting married, I think it would be nice if you and Noah made it a double wedding. You know, a reaffirmation of your vows."

"Ben and I agree with her. We would love to have a double wedding," Tabitha said. "You'll do it, won't you, Sirena?"

"I don't know," Sirena murmured, instinctively balking at the suggestion. Though Noah claimed he loved her, she wasn't sure she wanted him reminded of his last wedding day with the beautiful Cynthia by his side.

"Of course, we'll do it," Noah stated firmly.

"But, Noah," Sirena began as she looked up at him in frustration.

He leaned down and dropped a quick, hard kiss to her lips. "We got married by a justice of the peace before, Sirena. I think it would be a good idea to do it up right this time. Besides, it wouldn't hurt to have a few blessings from up above."

"Then it's settled," Ophelia said, already lapsing back into her tyrannical demeanor. She rose to her feet. "Come along, Pamela. Tabitha. We have two weddings to plan."

Before Sirena could make any further objections, they were gone.

"That wasn't fair, Noah. We should have discussed the wedding," she grumbled when he pulled her to her feet, sat down on her chair and settled her onto his lap.

"Well, it wasn't fair for you to announce that we'll be moving without discussing it with me. Particularly when I agree with Ophelia. You will be increasing your chances of an accident if you commute every day."

"You want to live in the mansion?" she asked in disbelief.

"Of course not. We will be moving. However, I'm going to relocate. My programs are being marketed nationally now, so where I'm headquartered doesn't matter," Noah said, refusing to acknowledge that nagging voice that reminded him of Ark II's problems. Relocation would financially tax him even further, perhaps even put him on the brink of bankruptcy. The voice also insisted that he tell Sirena about his problems; he cavalierly thrust it aside. He'd face that problem when he absolutely had to, not one minute before. He still had his pride.

"But what about your employees? You can't just put them out of work because of me."

Noah grinned, wondering how he could ever have considered her selfish and shallow. He found it endearing that her first thought was for his employees.

"I'll keep the retail part of the store open, Sirena. I'll offer the rest of them a chance to relocate with me. If they don't want to move, I'll give them a year's salary and a good recommendation."

Sirena released a sigh of relief. She would never have been able to live with herself if people had lost their jobs because Noah had an overprotective streak.

"Now, about the wedding," Noah said. "Why does it bother you?"

"No particular reason," Sirena mumbled.

"You're blushing, mermaid, which means you're lying."

"I'm not lying," she denied. "I'm hedging."

He caught her chin and forced her to look at him. "I love you, and I want a church wedding to reaffirm our vows. It's important to me, Sirena. Believe it or not, I'm a man of abiding faith. I want to hear those words, 'What God has joined together let no man put asunder.' Now, tell me why you object."

"It's not the ceremony that I object to, it's just that I keep remembering barging into that chapel and seeing your Cynthia standing there looking so beautiful. What if I don't measure up, Noah? You might take one look at me and decide that you've made a mistake."

Noah would have burst into laughter if she hadn't looked so somber and so vulnerable. He smiled as he brushed his knuckles against her blushing cheek.

"Sirena, the worst mistake I ever made in my life was letting you go two years ago. I should have given in to my instincts and come after you, but I let pride get in my way.

And as far as I'm concerned, no other woman in the world can measure up to you, because it's the beauty within you that I'm in love with. The outside package is only incidental."

"Oh, Noah," Sirena whispered as she gazed at him through misty eyes. "That's the most romantic thing I've ever heard."

"Good. Then the wedding is settled."

"You and Grandmother are like two peas from the same pod."

"I'm not sure I like that inference," Noah grumbled.

"It wasn't inference, it was a statement of fact," Sirena stated with a chuckle. Then she wrapped her arms around his neck and asked, "Did you really want to come after me two years ago?"

"I not only wanted to, but I actually spent the night at the end of your driveway a good number of times."

"You were at the mansion?" When he nodded, she said, "If you made it that far, what stopped you from coming the rest of the way?"

"Deep down inside I didn't think I was good enough for you," he confessed.

"Oh, you silly despot," she murmured as she leaned forward and kissed him.

"Sirena, does the lock work on your office door?" he murmured against her lips.

"Mmm, I don't know, but if it doesn't we can put Rufus on guard duty."

"I knew having a tiger around would prove to be handy."

IT WAS LATE AFTERNOON when Sirena slammed down the telephone and yelled for Margie. But instead of her administrative assistant responding to the summons, Noah walked into the room.

"Margie stepped out for a minute," he told her. "What's wrong?"

"Red tape!" Sirena railed as she tossed a handful of papers down on her desk in disgust. "I'm sick and tired of running around in circles like a trained dog."

Noah walked to her desk, picked up the papers and slid his glasses from the top of his head to his nose. After he'd scanned the paperwork and the notes she'd just taken from the telephone call, he asked, "Why did you buy a hotel?"

"That's what I've been asking myself," Sirena responded, looking disgruntled.

Noah dropped into a chair in front of her desk, stretched out his legs and patiently waited for a more direct answer to his question.

Sirena felt her ire waning as she propped her chin in her hands and gazed at him. During the past week she'd been wallowing in marital bliss, and not even the matrons, who were in continual battle over wedding preparations, could upset her for long.

"I bought the hotel so I could renovate it into apartments to use as a long-term shelter for the homeless who are skilled enough to find jobs. When you've been out on the streets, you don't make the best impression in an interview, and a lot of employers are reluctant to hire people who don't have a permanent address."

"In other words, you want to get them cleaned up, give them a decent place to eat and sleep and provide them with an address so that they'll appear to be stable members of the community," he commented thoughtfully.

"Exactly," Sirena said.

"Won't you be inviting in a group of freeloaders who have no intention of moving out?"

Sirena shook her head. "The tenants will be carefully screened to ensure that they're employable. They will sign a three-month lease, which will require them to work through our job placement services on a daily basis. If they turn down more than one job interview or refuse more than one job offer, they'll be evicted."

"You're going to throw them back out on the streets after putting a roof over their heads?" he asked doubtfully. "I know you too well, Sirena. You won't be able to do it."

"That's exactly why I'm going to stay completely out of the project. A board will be established that will consist of people with no association with the foundation, and they will listen to complaints of unfair treatment. Also, as an incentive for these people to get jobs and hold on to them, once they are hired the foundation will find them an apartment and pay their rent for one year, provided, of course, that they remain gainfully employed."

"That sounds pretty expensive. It could be a drain on your funds."

Sirena smiled complacently. "Actually, the matrons and my brothers have agreed to donate funds annually for the specific purpose of paying the rents."

Noah was truly shocked at that revelation. "I thought you'd purposely kept them out of the foundation to avoid interference."

"That was before this wonderful man burst into my life and convinced me that I could stand up to all of them. Since I can, I figured it was ridiculous not to hit them up for money."

It was Noah's turn to smile complacently. "I am proving handy to have around."

Sirena gave him a provocative look. "More than handy, Noah. In fact, in some areas of my life, you've become a downright necessity."

"Keep talking like that, mermaid, and I'll have to put Rufus back on guard duty," he murmured suggestively.

A quiver of excitement shot through Sirena, and she wondered how she'd ever managed to survive without him.

"So what's your problem with this hotel?" Noah asked, purposely ignoring the desire flickering in her eyes. It wasn't that he didn't want her. In fact, he wanted her every minute of every day, but they couldn't spend all of their time making love, even if the idea did sound appealing at the moment.

Sirena shook her head, pulling herself out of her sensual reverie. "Every time I turn around, another city inspector is giving me another list of renovations that must be made before they'll recommend licensure." She handed him the three previous lists and the corresponding contractors' reports to confirm that the changes had been made.

Noah frowned as he surveyed the documents. "You're right. You are getting the runaround. Do you know why?"

"No." She chuckled as she added, "Margie says it's a conspiracy. That these inspectors are getting a kickback to make me fed up so that I'll unload the place, and then some real estate mogul will snap up a renovated hotel for a song and make a fortune. She really does have an active imagination."

Noah shrugged. "Stranger things have happened, Sirena, but I agree that it's probably nothing more than some in-house politics. I made a few contacts at city hall when I did some work for them last year. Is it okay if I make a couple of calls and see what I can find out about this?"

Sirena regarded him pensively for a long moment. "You really have changed, Noah. Two years ago you wouldn't have asked, you'd have just done it."

"Two years ago, I was a fool," he stated dryly.

"You weren't a fool. You were just an infuriating despot."

He gave her a mock glare. "You'll pay for that one, Sirena."

"I'll look forward to it," she said with a bright laugh. "And, yes, please make your calls. If you can straighten out this mess, I'll be indebted to you forever."

"Now, that's an offer worth pursuing," he teased as he rose to his feet, leaned across her desk and dropped a kiss to her lips. "I'll try to have an answer for you tonight when you get home from your fund-raising committee meeting. Try not to be too late."

"Believe me, I plan on making this the shortest committee meeting in history. Try to avoid the matrons. Otherwise, you'll end up in the middle of an argument over the wedding preparations."

"Don't worry about me. Rufus and I talked about that early this morning, and we decided on a very long walk on the grounds tonight. Ben said he might even join us in order to stay out of the line of fire."

"I'm sorry they're being so difficult, Noah. If you want to change your mind about the wedding, I'll understand."

Something dangerous flashed in his eyes. "Have you changed your mind, Sirena?"

His words had been issued in a low challenge, but Sirena didn't even blink an eye. Somewhere along the way she'd begun to read between the lines with Noah. When he was behaving like this, it usually meant that he was feeling vulnerable.

She smiled. "No. In fact, if you decide to change yours, I may just drag you down the aisle kicking and screaming."

"You and what army?" he asked with a laugh, his good humor restored at the scene her words presented.

"Oh, I won't need an army," she responded complacently. "I'll just sic the matrons on you."

"Anything but that," Noah groaned expressively. "I promise I won't change my mind if you promise to keep the matrons chained up."

"You have my solemn word."

"I'll hold you to it. I'd better get out of here and make those calls." He'd just reached the doorway when he turned around. "By the way, my mother called a while ago and wants to know if we can come to a family reunion on Saturday. Are you free?"

The last remaining doubt of his love fled from Sirena's mind and she had to clear her throat to find her voice. "I'll make sure I'm free, Noah. I'm looking forward to meeting your family."

"Great. I'll give her a call." He threw her a kiss and disappeared.

Margie wandered in a few minutes later. "We'd better get going, boss. We don't want to have our moneybags patrons chomping at their designer pocketbooks because we're late."

"Sure," Sirena said with a dreamy sigh, still reveling in the fact that Noah was ready to introduce her to his family.

"My word, you're getting sappier by the day," Margie grumbled good-naturedly.

"I know," Sirena said as she rose to her feet and reached for her briefcase. "Love is grand, isn't it?"

NOAH ROLLED HIS EYES heavenward and muttered a prayer for five minutes of peaceful silence. Ophelia, Pamela and Tabitha had been arguing over the wedding reception throughout dinner. He was beginning to wonder if he had responded too hastily this afternoon when Sirena had offered him an out. He also wondered how she was managing to bear up under the strain, since he knew she was spending a good hour every night listening to this squabbling.

"We'll let Noah choose the entrée for the sit-down dinner," Ophelia suddenly announced, and Noah practically leaped under the table when their bright eyes all turned on him.

He cleared his throat uncomfortably and said, "I, uh, think you should probably consult with Sirena about this. After all, it's her wedding."

He knew he was taking the coward's way out and vowed that he'd make it up to his wife, who'd probably want to shoot him on sight, and justifiably so.

"Don't be ridiculous," Ophelia stated. "This is your wedding too, and a man has a better appreciation of food than a woman, anyway."

Noah arched a brow at that one, but refrained from comment. "I don't know much about sit-down dinners, Ophelia."

"You don't need to know about them. Just resolve this argument. I think we should serve beef as the entrée. Pamela thinks it should be seafood, and Tabitha doesn't care. Since you have to eat it, you can tell us what you prefer."

"Don't you think Ben should have a say in this?" Noah asked in an effort to gain some time. "I mean, this wedding was to be his and Tabitha's originally."

"Ben refuses to get involved in any of the wedding plans," Tabitha grumbled as she toyed with the small diamond in her engagement ring. "He says he values his life."

"Amen to that," Noah muttered lowly.

"Well, Noah?" Ophelia pressed.

He glanced toward Tabitha, ready to pass the ball on to her, but she shook her head. When he glanced toward

Pamela, he could see there wasn't going to be any help in that quarter, either.

"Why are we having a sit-down dinner?" he asked.

"Because it's tradition," Ophelia answered, "Barringtons always get married late in the afternoon, have a sit-down dinner and then dance all night."

"I see. I don't suppose we could break tradition by getting married in the early evening, have a huge buffet table with everything on it and dance all night."

"What a fabulous idea!" Tabitha exclaimed. "Mother, we could have a candlelight wedding. Wouldn't it be beautiful?"

"I think a candlelight wedding would be beautiful," Pamela stated. "It would also give us more time during the day to make sure everything is in order."

"True," Ophelia agreed with a thoughtful nod. Then, "It's settled. We'll have a candlelight wedding with a magnificent buffet. I'm glad I thought of it."

Noah knew he had to get out of the room before he burst out laughing; he excused himself and headed outside in search of Rufus. The tiger, elated at finally having his freedom, was rarely in sight, but he always sensed when it was Noah who stepped out the back door. Noah laughed when the big cat came bounding toward him and then plopped to the ground and rolled to his back so Noah could rub his silken stomach.

"I missed you today," Noah told him as he squatted and complied with the animal's request for a belly rub. "I also could have used your help a few minutes ago. Feel lucky that you never got married, old guy. What a mess."

"Does that mean you've changed your mind about the wedding?" Sirena asked as she stepped out the door behind him.

Noah, startled by her sudden appearance, nearly fell as he twisted around to see her. His eyes flew over her skimpy yellow top and even skimpier yellow shorts.

"You look like a beautiful daffodil. How long have you been home?"

Sirena shrugged. "Long enough to change, and long enough to eavesdrop on you and the matrons. You handled the menu problem quite well."

"You were listening and you didn't come to my rescue?" he growled as he surged to his feet and pulled her into his arms. "I'll get you for that."

Sirena giggled as she wrapped her arms around his neck. "I missed you."

"In that case, I forgive you. Let's take Rufus for a walk before the matrons discover you're home and kidnap you."

"That sounds wonderful," Sirena said with a weary sigh and leaned her head against his shoulder as they walked across the rolling lawns toward the stand of forested trees. Rufus lumbered ahead of them.

"How'd the meeting go?" he asked when he'd led her into the trees and out of sight of the house.

"It went very well. We've got some very innovative people on the committee this year, so we're coming up with some new ideas that I think will really pay off."

"Great. I've got some good news, too."

"Yeah, what?" she asked as she tilted back her head so she could gaze up to him.

"Hold on to your hat, mermaid, because as of tomorrow, your hotel will be licensed as a long-term shelter."

"Oh, Noah!" Sirena screamed as she threw her arms around his neck and kissed him exuberantly. "How did you do it?"

"Trade secret," he teased, feeling inordinately pleased that he'd managed to do something for her that her money couldn't buy. "Actually, I was right. There was some in-house politics going on, and you were just caught in the middle."

"I love you, Noah Samson," she declared as she gave him another exuberant kiss. But before Noah could deepen it, she danced away from him saying, "Margie and I need to get started on the project right away. If we work night and day, we can have the place open by early September. We'll have to order furniture, and appliances and—"

"Whoa," Noah said as he caught her around the waist and hauled her back into his arms. "Aren't you forgetting a couple of things?"

"Like what?" Sirena asked as she peered up at him in confusion.

"A wedding and a honeymoon."

Sirena blinked at him owlishly. "A honeymoon? You never said anything about a honeymoon."

"Some things are implied, mermaid."

"Couldn't we delay it? Just until after the shelter is open," she quickly added when he began to scowl.

For a moment Sirena's temper began to flare at his presumption that they'd run off on a honeymoon without even talking to her about it. She had obligations and she couldn't just drop everything at the foundation and run. But before she could work herself up into a furious dither some little inner voice reminded that she needed to get her priorities in order. The foundation and her good works were essential to her well-being, but Noah was her breath of life.

"A honeymoon sounds wonderful," she murmured, smiling as she watched his scowl disappear. Then she said thoughtfully, "In fact, it would probably be a lot more fun if I moved back into my room. If we practiced celibacy between now and the wedding, we would really appreciate a honeymoon."

"What!" Noah roared. "Are you crazy?"

"The idea doesn't appeal to you?" she asked as she batted her eyelids innocently.

"Just try leaving my bed," he stated in a tone that was a definite threat.

Sirena laughed as she hugged him tight. "I'm only joking, Noah."

"Well, your punch line stinks," he muttered as he hugged her back. "By the way, where do you want to go on your honeymoon?"

"Surprise me," Sirena said as she took his hand and began leading him back to the house, knowing that by now the matrons would be anticipating her arrival.

When they got to the back door, Noah turned her into his arms to kiss her, but the door opened and Ben said, "Mr. Noah, there's a Mr. Harding on the telephone for you. He says it's urgent."

Noah felt an instant surge of panic. John Harding was in charge of Ark II, and he'd only be calling if there was more trouble.

"Fine, Ben. Tell him I'll be right in."

He forced himself to remain relaxed as he dropped a peck to Sirena's lips. "Sorry, mermaid, but you know how these things are. Someone probably ordered five thousand pencils instead of five hundred pens, and now they need the boss to tell them what to do."

Sirena, sensing something was wrong, searched his face, but then dismissed the feeling when he appeared to be perfectly calm.

She nodded. "You take care of your pencils while I brave the matrons. If you haven't seen me in an hour, come to my rescue."

"I'll always come to your rescue, mermaid," he assured as he led her in the back door.

But who was going to come to his? he wondered. He had an ominous feeling that Noah's Ark was getting ready to collapse around his ears.

12

IT HAD BEEN YEARS since Noah had been to a formal gathering of his family, and he'd forgotten just how outdated his family's attitudes were. When his mother announced dinner and the men headed for the dining room to eat, while the women gathered the children and headed for the kitchen to have their repast, Noah knew he was in trouble. Sirena would kill him for not warning her about the family tradition of eating separately.

He found her in the kitchen, drew her aside and said, "Honey, I'm sorry. I'd forgotten about this or I would have warned you."

Sirena gave him a distantly amused smile. "Don't worry about it, Noah. Your sister-in-law Glenna has already explained the importance of the men being able to eat in peace and quiet so they can solve all the family's problems." When Noah looked grim, she grinned, leaned forward and whispered, "I can't wait for the men in your family to meet the matrons. We're going to have one humdinger of a wedding."

"You know, mermaid, sometimes your sense of humor is downright sick," he muttered.

She chuckled, raised on tiptoe and brushed her lips against his. Then she pushed him toward the dining room and joined the women in their efforts to feed twenty-three rowdy children, ranging in age from mere weeks to fourteen years.

When she and Noah first arrived, she'd felt like a bug in a jar under the family's wary scrutiny. But then Noah's grandfather had welcomed her, and from that moment on Sirena had been accepted. She decided that she couldn't have felt more at home if she'd been born into the family, and she hugged that knowledge to her, rejoicing in it.

Noah on the other hand, had never felt more separated from his family as he sat at the table and listened to his grandfather, father, brothers and brothers-in-law discuss their farming operations, and the problems inherent to their profession. Since he had nothing to contribute to the conversation, he became introspective worrying about his own business problems.

Ark II simply wasn't taking off the way he'd expected, and he still couldn't figure out why. If he couldn't generate interest in the program to recover the funds he'd invested, there was no way he could relocate to Harrisburg. In fact, he might be forced to do some delving into his private savings, which could definitely cause a problem with buying a house so he and Sirena could move out of the Barrington mansion. All in all, everything was in a veritable mess, and he had to find a way out of it.

His grandfather's voice pulled him out of his thoughts, and Noah glanced toward him. "I'm sorry, Grandfather. I didn't hear your question."

Josiah Samson was in his eighties, but his mind was as sharp as ever, and he still had the physical strength to volunteer his time at the blacksmith shop in Old Bedford Village. The old man was imperious, and Noah felt like an errant schoolboy beneath his piercing gaze.

To make matters worse, Noah's father and his four brothers and four brothers-in-law had all centered their attention on him. Since Noah was the youngest of the family, he'd always been at the end of the pecking order, which was one of the reasons why he'd left Bedford and gone to Maryland. He loved his family too deeply to risk a permanent rift in order to declare his independence. Distance guaranteed autonomy.

"I asked you to explain the meaning of this upcoming wedding. If you and your wife are married, it seems that a wedding is only a waste of money," the old man stated with asperity.

Noah realized several things about himself in that moment. The first was that he could still, even after all these years, slip back into the roll of subservience to his elders, and everyone in the Samson family was his elder. He also hated the fact that the men in his family never referred to their women by name, but always in terms of ownership, such as my wife, your wife, my daughter, your daughter. Finally, he understood that he'd grown beyond them. The realization made him feel proud and innately sad at the same time.

"Sirena and I are married," he answered, aware that he'd purposely broken family tradition by calling his wife by name. He decided to take it one step further by stating, "I don't see any reason to explain our upcoming wedding, and if we want to waste our money, it's our right. All you have to worry about is whether or not you're going to come."

The silence around the table was emphasized by the laughter and lively conversation that drifted in from the kitchen. Noah shifted his gaze from his grandfather to his father, and from him to each and every one of his brothers and brothers-in-law. It was a tacit challenge, and he was both surprised and pleased to discover that none of them seemed willing to take him up on it.

It was his father who finally broke the silence by sighing heavily and saying, "We'll all be there."

"We'll be expecting you," Noah said as he rose to his feet and lifted his plate, deciding that the mood in here was too somber for his taste. He wanted to hear laughter, in particular the bright, tinkling laugh of his wife. "I'm sure you'll all excuse me. Since I haven't been home in a very long while, I'd like to spend some time reacquainting myself with my nieces and nephews. I think I'll join them for dinner."

With that, he headed for the kitchen, deciding that he rather enjoyed breaking tradition.

SIRENA KEPT EYEING NOAH surreptitiously as they drove back to Harrisburg. They'd already completed half of the three-hour drive, and outside of answering when she spoke to him, he'd been silent.

"Noah, is something wrong?" she finally asked.

He glanced toward her and smiled. "Of course not. Why?"

"You just seem awfully quiet."

He shrugged as he turned his eyes back on the road. "I've just been doing a little soul-searching."

A small tingle of fear centered itself in Sirena's lower back. She tried to sound nonchalant when she asked, "Discover anything interesting?"

"Only that I love you more than I did a minute ago, and twice as much as the minute before that," he said as he caught her hand and brought it to his lips.

The tingle of fear faded away. "I didn't do anything wrong today, did I? I did my very best not to offend anyone."

"You did fine," he answered as he swung his gaze toward her, his eyes glowing with approval. "and even if you had offended someone, you would have been justified. The matrons are saints when compared to the Samson patriarchs."

"Well, I don't know if I'd go that far," Sirena demurred. "I think they're six of one and half a dozen of the other."

"Maybe," Noah stated. He was silent for several more miles before he said, "During the past few weeks I've realized just how miserable I was to you two years ago, and it shocked me. At first I couldn't understand my behavior, because in retrospect, it was out of character. But as I watched my family interact today, I found myself falling back into the old pattern and it dawned on me that when I first met you, I'd just spent the past six weeks in the bosom of my family."

"You'd become a Samson again," she murmured thoughtfully.

He flashed her a grin. "Right. An old-fashioned, straitlaced, uptight, chauvinistic despot."

"And I responded to you in the same way that I responded to the overprotective, didactic matrons," she stated in understanding, "I screamed instead of talked."

"It would be interesting to know what would have happened if we'd met each other under other circumstances, wouldn't it?"

"No," Sirena said as she smiled at him. "I love you for what you are, Samson, despot and all. I think I had to fall in love with that side of you, before I could truly love the man that you are today."

Noah felt himself feeling uncustomarily sappy as he caught her hand, refusing to let it go until they reached Harrisburg and the traffic demanded that he do so.

SIRENA WAS EXHAUSTED. She'd not only put in a ten-hour day at the office, but she'd spent most of the night addressing wedding invitations. Her feet hurt, her back ached, and her fingers were cramped when she let herself into the bedroom she shared with Noah.

She frowned when she found the room empty, but realized he was on the balcony when she saw the curtains billowing. She slipped through them but stopped when she saw Noah leaning against the railing, his shoulders slumped.

In the past week she'd sensed that something was wrong, though whenever she asked, he'd denied her assertion. Until this very moment, she hadn't been convinced that he was lying, but now she was. She moved toward him.

"What's wrong, Noah?" she questioned when she perched her elbows on the railing beside his. "And don't say it's nothing," she added before he could respond. "I'm your wife. You owe me the truth."

Every male instinct Noah had rebelled at her words, but he forced himself to think his way through them before he answered. Finally, he decided that she was right. She was his wife, and she did deserve the truth, even if he found it untenable.

He stared out over the sprawling acres of the Barrington mansion, which were lit by moonlight and streetlights.

"My new computer program isn't selling," he told her, "and I can't figure out why. It's a breakthrough in the technology. It will not only mate with any software program in existence, but it will enhance it. It's so simple that anyone who can turn on a computer can not only use it, but answer simple questions that will allow them to design a program to fit their own needs."

"That's the program you put in at the foundation!" Sirena exclaimed. She'd been amazed at how simple the program was, and astonished at how easily it had adapted to their needs.

Noah nodded.

"Don't worry about it," Sirena said then. "In time it's going to take off and you won't be able to keep up with the orders."

He turned and leaned his hip against the railing so he could see her better. "I can't relocate Noah's Ark until half the stock is sold, Sirena. I also don't see how we can buy a house until that happens. I'm not in desperate straits yet, but I'm close to it."

Sirena refrained from pointing out that she could not only finance his relocation, but buy any house they were interested in. He might not be the quintessential Samson, but he wasn't so far removed that he wouldn't be offended by her offer. In the past several weeks she'd discovered that she liked his stubborn pride, because there was an essential part of her that identified with it.

"Well, I think that we can compromise until you're back on your feet. You still have your condo, and we'll always be welcome here. We can work out our schedules so that we spend half our time in Hagerstown and half our time in Harrisburg."

"That wouldn't be fair to you," Noah said. "You're working hard to get your hotel open. You can't afford time away from the project."

Sirena shifted her hip to the railing and reached up to touch his cheek. "You're more important to me than any project, Noah."

He grasped her hand and held it against his lips. "I feel as if I'm failing you, mermaid."

"You're only facing a temporary downturn. It'll work itself out."

"And if it doesn't?" he inquired as he raised haunted eyes to her face. "I need to succeed for you."

"You already have," she stated fervently. "I don't need air as much as I need you. When are you going to accept that fact?"

Noah swept her into his arms and buried his face in her hair. He wanted to believe all her words, but he had enough Samson left inside him to proclaim that even though he couldn't match her in money, he had to at least have enough to take care of her. Right now he was about as solvent as the Confederate states at the end of the Civil War.

When her lips found his, he lifted her into his arms and carried her to bed, where he made love to her desperately, urgently. It didn't take his fears away, but her response to him helped him hold them at bay. She loved him for better or for worse. However, he still thought he'd be better able to cope with it if they weren't starting out with the worst.

Sirena pretended sleep when Noah left her and returned to the balcony. She had to do something to help him, but what? She knew in her heart that he'd never accept money from her, even if it was offered in the form of a loan.

She lay in bed, feeling lonely and bereft, until she finally realized that there was one act that she could perform. She could call in some Barrington favors by contacting friends with businesses who she felt could benefit from his computer program. After all, she used it at the foundation, and she knew exactly what the program had to offer. She could extol its virtues through her own experience.

Noah didn't return to bed for several hours, and Sirena lay curled up beneath the covers as she laid out her plan. She had drifted off to sleep before Noah returned, but she did so with a relieved mind. If she had her way Noah's Ark would be flourishing within a week. She ignored the little voice inside that kept insisting that before she carried out her plan she had to discuss it with Noah.

She wasn't doing anything wrong, she concluded. She was only going to do for him what he had done for her when he'd helped her get her hotel licensed. Make a few calls to a few contacts. When the voice promptly reminded that he'd asked for her permission to make his calls, she shrugged it off, telling herself that the circumstances were not the same.

NOAH WAS FLYING HIGH. Interest in Ark II had exploded. His staff had been receiving phone call after phone call, and for every sale they made, they received at least one more referral. When Ben opened the door for him, he was grinning from ear to ear.

"You must have had a good day, Mr. Noah," Ben stated.

"Absolutely marvelous," Noah answered as he strode through the door and clapped the older man on the back. "Are you ready for tonight's engagement party?"

Ben chuckled. "As ready as I'll ever be. Tabitha, however, is a nervous wreck."

It was Noah's turn to chuckle as he solemnly stated, "Women."

Ben actually grinned. "Speaking of women, your wife's upstairs. She came home early to get ready for the party."

"Thanks," Noah said as he headed for the stairs, eager to share his news with Sirena.

But Ark II's success was the last thing on his mind when he found her in the bathtub floating in bubbles.

"Welcome home," she told him with a smile. "How did your day go?"

"Fantastic," he murmured, unable to tear his eyes away from the water that lapped at her breasts. When it finally provided him with a brief glimpse of her nipples, he began to shed his suit. "It was also long, tiring, and the air-conditioning in my car went on the fritz. Like some company?"

"I think there's room enough in here for two," she murmured as he sat on the toilet, pulled off his socks and then dropped his pants.

"I love you," he said when he stepped into the tub a moment later.

Sirena let her gaze flow up the length of his body, thrilled by the obvious evidence of his words.

"Show me," she whispered throatily.

He responded with a deep groan as he lowered himself over her, and she wrapped her arms and legs around him in welcome.

"I missed you," she whispered as he caught her lips in a brief, teasing kiss.

"Then show me," he demanded on a male growl of satisfaction.

Sirena gladly obeyed the order, and by the time she was done, the bathroom floor was flooded and there wasn't a bubble left in the tub.

Later, as they dressed for Ben and Tabitha's engagement party, Noah regaled Sirena with Ark II's sudden success. She smiled indulgently as she listened. Again that little voice inside nagged at her, insisting that she tell him about her calls, but he was so happy, and she knew instinctively that he wouldn't respond well to the news. They were getting along so well that she didn't want to argue with him, and she soothed her conscience by promising herself she'd break the news to him later. Much later, she amended when Noah scooped her into his arms and treated her to a kiss that was guaranteed to make them late for the engagement party. Much, much later.

NOAH SMILED as he watched Sirena talk animatedly with a group of people across the room. His entire world was rosy, and he couldn't keep his eyes off the woman he loved. It wouldn't take much provocation for him to drag her out of here, take her home and ravish her.

But they had years ahead of them to indulge in that pastime, and tonight was Tabitha and Ben's night to celebrate. He knew how important it was to Sirena to share in it.

"Why, Noah, how are you?"

Noah swiveled his head toward the voice and smiled in recognition of William Davis, one of his newest clients who'd purchased Ark II.

"Bill," he said. "I didn't know you'd be here tonight."

"I'm an old friend of the Barrington family. I understand that you're married to Sirena."

Noah nodded as his eyes drifted back toward the crowd. He smiled as he watched Sirena approach them. She looked gorgeous in the shimmering turquoise dress that clung to her curves.

"Bill!" Sirena exclaimed as she went into William Davis's arms. "I'm so happy you could come."

"I wouldn't miss Tabitha's engagement party. You know that I've always thought of her as a sister," the older man told her as he hugged her and then pushed her back so that he could look at her. He gave an approving nod. "You look beautiful, as always. Your father would be proud."

Sirena blushed and slid her arm around Noah's waist. "I assume you've met my husband, Noah Samson," she said. "Noah, this is Bill Davis. He was my father's best friend."

"Bill and I have been doing business together," Noah stated. "He just bought Ark II for his company."

Bill nodded in acknowledgment of Noah's words. "I want to thank you for telling me about that program, Sirena. My staff had discussed it, but dismissed it, because they were sure it couldn't live up to its claims. If you hadn't called, we'd never have taken a chance on it."

At Bill's words, Sirena's smile became as stiff as Noah's body against hers, and she gave a jerky nod of her head. "I'm glad it worked out for you, Bill."

Bill grinned widely and gave Noah a sly wink. "Hang on to this plum, son. With Sirena's contacts, she'll make you a millionaire overnight." He glanced around the crowd. "My wife is out there somewhere. I'd better go find her. You two take care."

"Yes," Sirena responded with a brittle smile, knowing that if Noah's body had been stiff before, it was now rigid. "We'll do that. Hope you can make the wedding."

"Debra and I will be there with bells on."

When he was gone, Sirena risked a glance up at Noah, and though she'd expected to meet a glower, she wasn't prepared for the ice-cold gleam in his eyes.

"Noah—" she began, only to have him interrupt rudely.

"Just shut up, Sirena."

He grabbed her arm and hauled her toward the door of the opulent country club.

"Noah, we can't leave," she protested, and shivered under the murderous look he centered on her.

She snapped her mouth shut as he dragged her out the door and all but threw her into his car. He was more furious than she'd ever seen him, and she cowered in her seat when he climbed in beside her. He didn't say a word. She grimaced when he shoved his car into first, grinding the gears.

That inner voice that had been railing at Sirena now began to crow with an "I told you so." But she refused to accept its prediction of doom. Noah was furious, and she didn't blame him. She'd gone behind his back to help him, but once his temper cooled, he'd understand. He did love her, after all, and she'd done what she'd done out of love.

It was only after they'd reached the mansion and he'd hauled her upstairs to their room that he finally spoke.

"Just what in hell did you think you were doing when you told your friends to buy my program?" he demanded in a voice that didn't vibrate with one ounce of love.

Sirena nervously twisted her hands together. "I didn't tell them to buy, Noah. I simply told them that the program was so wonderful that they should check it out." When he didn't respond, but continued to glare at her, she said, "You should be glad I can help you, Noah. I'm your wife. When you succeed, I succeed."

"Help me?" Noah questioned disparagingly. "You made me look like a business cuckold!"

"I did no such thing!" Sirena railed at the accusation. "I simply promoted your program."

"You told your friends to buy it!"

"I didn't tell them to buy it," she again denied. "I told them to check into it."

"It's the same thing, Sirena. You used the Barrington name to promote Ark II. You didn't have any faith in me, and you weren't about to let the world know that you were married to a failure."

"Noah, you're overreacting to this entire situation," she stated with a calmness she didn't feel.

"Overreacting?!" he bellowed. "My wife makes me look like an idiot, and she says I'm overreacting? Well, I'm through, Sirena. We're through."

"What does that mean?" she asked, trying to ignore the cold shiver of fear that engulfed her.

"I'm getting the hell out of here," he announced as he walked to the closet, hauled out his suitcase and began to throw his clothes inside. "Have Jonathan Harcourt contact me in the morning. I'll sign whatever I have to sign to end this marriage as soon as possible."

"Noah, you don't mean that!" Sirena exclaimed as she grabbed his arm, causing him to drop the armful of underwear he'd just pulled out of the bureau.

He shook off her arm and bent to retrieve his clothing. "I mean it, Sirena. It's over."

Sirena's eyes filled with tears, but she blinked them back, determined not to cry now. She didn't need tears, but words that would reinstate sanity.

"But we've worked too hard to rebuild! You said you loved me!"

He straightened, his arms once again filled with his clothes, and Sirena's knees shook when he leveled his blue eyes on her. They were filled with more than hate. They were filled with abhorrence.

"Get out of my way, Sirena. I will not have people insinuating that I live off my wife."

Sirena wanted to rail at him, scream at him, but she forced herself to remain calm. The rest of her life depended on this moment, and she wasn't going to lose everything over a wounded male ego.

"I will admit that I was wrong to call my friends without talking to you," she said as she watched him toss his underwear into his suitcase and head for the closet. "But I was only helping you, just like you helped me when you got the hotel licensed."

"It's not the same," he snapped as he hauled out an armful of suits and threw them into the suitcase.

"It is the same, Noah," she said, catching him as he headed back toward the closet and forcing him to face her. "A marriage is a team effort. You do what you can to help your mate. If you can't accept that, then everything we've spent the past month working for hasn't been worth it. We've come so far. Are you willing to throw it all away simply because I've stepped on your pride?"

For a moment she was convinced she'd reached him. His expression changed and grew introspective. She held her breath, waiting for him to reach the natural conclusion. She'd been wrong, but she'd been wrong for all the right reasons. If he truly loved her, he had to recognize that fact.

But all her hopes were dashed when his eyes changed again, growing even colder than before. "You're right," he drawled cruelly. "Everything we've spent the past month working for hasn't been worth it. Just get out, Sirena, and let me leave in peace. If I had one ounce of intelligence, I would have never come here in the first place. I would have let you have your divorce and married Cynthia."

"You don't mean that, Noah," she stated calmly, though there wasn't one cell in her body that felt calm. "When you cool down, you'll feel differently."

His lips curved into that satyr's grin that had captured her heart that first day she met him. But the grin wasn't reflected in his eyes, and his voice was colder than an Arctic wind.

"Get out of my way, Sirena. I need to finish packing."

Sirena's eyes burned and her throat ached as she watched him finish filling his suitcase and close the lid.

He cast a glance around the room and said, "If I've forgotten anything, mail it to me C.O.D. Goodbye, Sirena."

It was only when he walked out and slammed the door behind him that Sirena let her tears begin to fall. She'd driven away the man she loved by trying to help him. She kept telling herself that if he couldn't understand her motivation, then he wasn't worth this ache inside. It didn't help. It only made her cry harder.

"MOTHER, WOULD YOU please just go away," Sirena groaned from her bed as her mother opened the curtains covering Sirena's sliding glass doors, letting in a blinding ray of sunshine.

"No," Pamela stated as she turned to face her daughter. "We have a million details to finalize about the wedding and we need your help."

"Noah is gone, and he isn't coming back," Sirena said stoutly, as she sat up in bed and glowered at her mother.

They'd been having the same argument for two days, and Pamela seemed oblivious to Sirena's pronouncement. "He packed his underwear, Mother," she added when Pamela continued to give her a vapid smile.

"Anyone in love with a Barrington can never turn their back on them," Pamela stated as she opened Sirena's closet and hauled out a dressing gown. "He'll be back. Just get dressed, come down to breakfast and help us decide on the flowers."

"Mother!"

But Sirena's protest went unheeded as Pamela exited, closing the door quietly behind her.

"This is crazy," Sirena muttered. She climbed out of bed and headed for her closet, but not to don a dressing gown.

What she needed, she decided, was a day at the office. She eyed her wardrobe. It was time she got back to the foundation and got on with her life.

She kept telling herself that she wasn't going to wear black, even if she did feel as if she were in mourning. In fact, maybe she'd go for red, she decided, as she reached for the one outrageous garment in her closet that was a blood-red.

No, it was too dressy for the office. She tossed it aside, reaching instead for a nice black wool sheath. It was too somber and too warm for the season, but a heat rash might be just what she needed to drag her out of her doldrums.

She was still contemplating the dress as she called out an irritated "Come in" at the knock on her door.

"Hello, Sirena," a deep voice drawled.

She spun around, her eyes wide in disbelief. "Noah." Her voice would have sounded breathless, except it was far too weak for even that description.

He nodded, leaned back against the door and stared at her. "You look like hell."

"Thank you," she said irritably. "However, I didn't ask for your opinion. Forget something in your hurry to move out?"

"Yes," Noah answered as his blue eyes skimmed down her. "You've lost weight."

"Don't be ridiculous. You've only been gone two days."

He nodded. "Two damnably miserable days, and you have lost weight."

She lifted her chin a defiant notch. "I've been ill. I'm probably dehydrated. What did you forget?"

"You."

She refused to meet his eyes and concentrated on the dress in her hand. It was the only way to keep her knees from buckling.

"What does that mean?" she asked, wanting to sound casual, but deciding she sounded desperate. It made her temper flare.

Noah released a heavy sigh when she refused to look at him. He decided that right now she probably hated him, and he couldn't blame her. He didn't agree with what she'd done to him, but he did understand her motivation. She loved him and she'd wanted to help him.

"I've done a lot of thinking during the past two days," he told her.

"And?" she asked sulkily.

"And I've come to the conclusion that you're right. In order to make our marriage work, we have to function as a team. However, Sirena, you shouldn't have gone behind my back."

Sirena opened her mouth to defend herself, but closed it when Noah raised his hand for silence.

"I already know what you're going to say. I would have turned down your offer of help if you'd come to me. I'm a Samson at heart, and I always will be, which means I have a major problem when it comes to pride. A Samson doesn't live off his wife in any way, shape or form. What you did to me put my pride on the line, even if you did it for all the right reasons."

"I'd do it again," she said, raising her chin another defiant notch.

His lips twitched, even if he didn't give in to a full-fledged grin. "I know that. That's why I love you. You see, my sweet mermaid, I finally understood what it was all about. And you're right. It's team effort. You'll fight for my success, just as I'll fight for yours. I also realized that no success will mean anything if I can't share it with you."

When she didn't respond, but continued to stare at her abominable dress, he said, "I love you, Sirena. I want you to be my wife. For better or for worse. For richer or for poorer. Until death do us part."

"Oh, Noah," she whispered as her hand became limp and the dress dropped to her feet.

Noah was at her side instantly, his arms around her securely. "Say you love me," he demanded as his lips found hers in urgent persuasion.

"I love you," she repeated by rote, unable to get close enough to him.

"Does this mean the wedding's still on?" he rasped, swinging her up into his arms.

"That depends," Sirena answered throatily as she wound her arms around his neck.

"On what?" he demanded hoarsely. He dropped her to the mattress and stretched over her.

"I want to spend our honeymoon at your cabin. I've been dying to know what it would be like to make love on your rose petal-covered bed."

Noah's grin curled her toes and melted every bone in her body. "You've got yourself a deal, mermaid. One hell of a deal."

COMING NEXT MONTH

A compelling novel of deadly revenge and passion
from Harlequin's bestselling international
romance author Penny Jordan

POWER PLAY

Eleven years had passed but the
terror of that night was something
Pepper Minesse would never
forget. Fueled by revenge against
the four men who had brutally
shattered her past, she set in
motion a deadly plan to destroy
their futures.

Available in February!

 Harlequin Books®

HPP-